ISLAND OF GRAVES

GWYN BENNETT

Storm

This is a work of fiction. Names, characters, business, events and incidents are the products of the author's imagination. Any resemblance to actual persons, living or dead, or actual events is purely coincidental.

Copyright © Gwyn Bennett, 2024

The moral right of the author has been asserted.

All rights reserved. No part of this book may be reproduced or used in any manner without the prior written permission of the copyright owner.

To request permissions, contact the publisher at rights@stormpublishing.co

Ebook ISBN: 978-1-80508-354-2
Paperback ISBN: 978-1-80508-356-6

Cover design: Eileen Carey
Cover images: Shutterstock, iStock

Published by Storm Publishing.
For further information, visit:
www.stormpublishing.co

ALSO BY GWYN BENNETT

The Dr Harrison Lane Mysteries

1. *Broken Angels*
2. *Beautiful Remains*
3. *Deadly Secrets*
4. *Innocent Dead*
5. *Perfect Beauties*
6. *Captive Heart*
7. *Winter Graves*
8. *Dark Whispers*

Saskia Monet Series

1. *The Stolen Ones*
2. *Secrets in the Blood*
3. *Island of Graves*

The DI Clare Falle Series

1. *Lonely Hearts*
2. *Home Help*
3. *Death Bond*

The Villagers

Dead End

PROLOGUE
SUNDAY

The air hung with autumn. Base undertones of ripe blackberries and decaying leaves were jazzed up with the sweet scent of flowering ivy, heavy and trapped in the damp air. Doug Langlois had climbed the slope from La Blinerie, puffing a little more than he'd have liked and wishing he hadn't succumbed to a second sausage roll. It was all probably a wasted journey anyway. Someone had emailed the Jersey Heritage offices, and they'd passed it on to the archaeology section of the Société Jersiaise, which was how it had found its way to him. *Looks like someone has dug up the ground inside Le Dolmen du Mont Ubé*, it read.

They'd had vandalism before now, and a few years previous someone had been trying to extract crystals from the stones at another dolmen in the island. Mindless idiots who didn't understand the significance of the ancient monuments which had stood for thousands of years as a record of humanity. It made his blood boil. This most recent report could be malicious, but Doug's money was actually on a dog. The site had plenty of dog walkers passing close by it and dogs loved to scrabble in the earth where rabbits or other vermin had left their scent.

At least it had got him out the house. He loved autumn, almost as much as he loved spring and the rebirth after winter. Summer could be hit or miss. Too hot or sometimes just disappointing. Autumn though, was almost a spiritual time of year, when the old guard in the natural world made way for the new blood which would come out in spring. Bees, wasps and other insects went into hibernation, their new queens prepared to emerge once winter has finished its reign. The old queens and the workers would be spent; their wings no longer beating and their bodies rotting down with the rest of the natural mulch. It was the same with the trees and plants, a time for hunkering down and sleeping as the days got shorter and the air colder.

Doug felt like that himself some years, especially since he'd retired. It was one reason he volunteered with the Société and probably also why he always put on a few pounds at this time – back to thinking about that extra sausage roll again. He burped a greasy sausagey burp just as the granite stones of the dolmen came into sight.

The Neolithic passage grave consisted of large pink granite stones weathered and patterned with grey lichen, standing upright like irregular teeth in a bottom jaw. From where Doug stood, the stones only looked to be a couple of feet tall, but that was deceptive. The grave was sunken and their true height of around five and a half feet only showed itself when you stepped down into the now open chamber. When it was built it was probably covered by an earth mound, but now it was sadly unprotected from dogs, vandals and the elements. It might not have quite the same visual impact as Stonehenge, but it was nonetheless an important ritual site from around six thousand years ago.

Doug approached the dolmen from the public footpath and peered over the top of the first row of stones into the chamber. It was then that it hit him. A career spent in the police force and a keen sense of smell meant Doug recognised the odour immediately. Nobody ever forgot that stench.

He instantly switched into professional mode, scanning the ground. It was clear somebody had indeed disturbed the earth and random clumps of grass, although there'd been a reasonable attempt to put the turf back on top again. Question was, what had been buried? The disturbed area was about four feet in length, probably some mourning dog owner who'd decided to bury their favourite fur baby in a place where they had happy memories. Very sweet, but it was vandalism. Disturbing an archaeological site of significance like this couldn't be tolerated. Fido would have to be dug back up and the burial chamber checked for any signs the digging had caused subsidence or damage.

Doug walked round to the opening, looking for a large stick as he went, with which to poke at the earth. Before he reported the incident, he needed to double-check what was in there. With any luck, they might be able to track the perpetrator down quite quickly if they'd posted about their loss on the Jersey Dog Forum page on Facebook. Doug didn't have anything against canines – they'd had their much-loved Labrador, Lucy, for thirteen years, but nobody had an excuse to disturb an archaeological site like this.

From the smell, Doug guessed that the person who'd interred their beloved pet hadn't dug a particularly deep hole. No doubt hampered by the naturally found granite, as well as any that had been brought to the site by their forebears; plus, there was a house and garden close by the site. Perhaps they'd been disturbed.

He stooped down and started to scrape at the loosened topsoil, flinging a sod of grassy earth to one side and attempting to clear a small area in the middle of the disturbed section. He expected to see fur, or perhaps a cloth that the unfortunate animal had been wrapped in.

After just a few minutes, a dirty pink fabric could be seen, just a couple of inches below the surface. Doug tried to pull at the fabric using the stick, to see if it unwrapped, but it wouldn't budge. He sighed. The smell was really quite unpleasant now, all the aroma of autumn and the sweet ivy flowers had been smothered by the rotting carcass. He was getting impatient. Already annoyed by whoever had done this, he scraped away more of the earth in an attempt to get a proper identification.

At first, he thought it was some kind of a plant root. Pale, muddy, and tinged with green and black, it protruded from the dark earth. Then he saw a fingernail and realised there were others, and almost immediately, that they were attached to a hand. Doug nearly fell backwards in his haste. Despite his thirty-six-year police career, he'd never had the misfortune of coming across and viewing a buried corpse before.

As Doug reached for his mobile phone and scrambled out of the grave chamber, his body finally rejected the greasy sausage rolls in one violent surge. It was going to be embarrassing explaining that to his former colleagues.

ONE

SUNDAY

Detective Inspector Winter Labey had just finished his roast beef Sunday lunch, including some especially nice crunchy roast potatoes, courtesy of his mother. He was sat at his parents' dining table talking about Asian hornets. His mother had made blackberry and apple crumble for dessert but had been forced to pick the berries away from where she usually got them, as somebody had found an Asian hornet nest in the brambles.

'Damed things are all over,' his father was saying. 'The volunteer trackers are doing a good job, they've found hundreds of nests, but one day someone's going to get badly stung by those things.'

'Not to mention what they're doing to our bees and the other pollinators,' his mother joined in. 'You should see how quickly they can destroy a hive.'

'We're going to put a trap out in the garden in the spring, catch any of the new queens that come out,' his dad said. 'Do our bit for the environment.'

'That's good. Jonno had one in his beer the other day. Big things they are,' Winter added.

'Well your mother braved the hornets and the brambles to

pick some blackberries, didn't you, love?' His father smiled appreciatively at his mother, who was walking back in from the kitchen with oven gloves wrapped around a dish of bubbling crumble.

'Yes, my friend Enid and I went together so we could help each other. We must have picked about six pounds of berries between us. Do you remember when you used to come picking blackberries with me?' she said to Winter. 'Used to be one for the pot and one for your mouth.' She raised her eyebrows at him. 'Enid and I were a little more efficient at picking. Never understand why more people don't collect blackberries, they're full of vitamin C, delicious, *and* they're free.'

'People are just too lazy these days,' his dad offered, 'would rather buy a plastic punnet of something that's probably already lost most of its goodness anyway, from the supermarket.'

'Watch your mouths, it's just come out the oven and is very hot,' Winter's mother warned as she placed a bowl of the blackberry and apple crumble in front of him.

'Thanks, Mum,' he said, reaching for the cream and the custard. 'Think I'll have a bit of both.'

Winter went for Sunday lunch at his parents' at least once a month. He knew his mother enjoyed being able to still cook for him, and it gave him a good opportunity to catch up with his parents. When he had a big case on, the lunches usually had to be postponed, but since the Cabot murders, it had been relatively quiet. They were still working on that case as it hadn't gone to trial yet, but the pressure was off: they had their killer.

The only other outstanding murder was that of Allan Hall, who'd been found floating off the coast with a stab wound to the back of his neck. Everything had pointed to the boyfriend, Kevin Baker, and he'd been charged, but Winter wasn't a hundred per cent convinced they'd cracked that one. He'd found himself in a minority of one with that view though, so he'd put it on the back burner until all the evidence was collected.

Winter had just put his first mouthful of blackberry and apple crumble in his mouth, when his phone rang.

'It's my work phone, sorry,' he apologised to his parents and stepped away from the table.

'DI Labey, sorry to interrupt your Sunday,' said the voice on the other end, which he recognised to be Detective Constable Peter Edwards. He'd obviously drawn the short straw for being on duty over the weekend. 'We've got a buried body up at the Mont Ubé dolmen.'

'At the dolmen? When you say body, are we talking bones or fresh?'

'Unfortunately fresh, or at least sometime in the last few weeks.'

'OK, have forensics and the pathologist been informed?'

'Yes. I'm up here now and we're closing off the surrounding area to secure the site.'

Winter sighed. He knew things had been too quiet. 'OK, I'll be with you about half an hour.'

The look on his parents' faces when he returned to the lunch table told him they'd already guessed he wouldn't be staying for any after-lunch conversation.

'Sorry,' he said to them.

'You not even going to finish your crumble?' his mother asked.

'Damned right I am,' he replied and picked up his bowl, wolfing down the deep purple dessert. If he was going to go into work then he needed his energy.

'Want me to put you some in a Tupperware for later? There's too much for us to finish,' his mum offered.

'You two will finish it off surely, won't you?' Winter half-heartedly suggested, but was pleased to see he wasn't persuasive enough because his mother disappeared off to the kitchen to sort him out a portion.

'I hope that boss of yours appreciates you,' his dad said to him, in between mouthfuls of his own crumble.

Winter doubted that Detective Chief Inspector Christopher Sharpe appreciated anything about him at all, but he didn't say that to his dad. 'Of course, Dad, everyone pulls their weight, it's not just me.'

Winter was true to his word and arrived at the crime scene half an hour after speaking to DC Edwards. That is one advantage in Jersey, nowhere was really very far on the nine by five miles island. He had a full belly of lunch, and a Tupperware of crumble on his passenger seat, and felt the added lunchtime burden as he began the climb up Mont Ubé from La Blinerie. It wasn't a particularly large hill, but with an ample helping of roast lunch and crumble, he felt decidedly sluggish.

He signed in with the officer manning the crime scene cordon, pleased to see that protocols were being followed. DC Edwards was reliable; he'd obviously secured the scene as best as he could because as Winter arrived on the footpath adjacent to the dolmen, he could see other officers manning the cordon on the other side where the footpath led to Nicolle Tower.

'Sir,' DC Edwards addressed him formally in the company of their uniformed colleagues, and came forward ready to brief him. 'A Société Jersiaise archaeology volunteer arrived to investigate a report that the ground inside the burial chamber had been disturbed. He thought it might have been a dog digging, then suspected a canine burial, but stopped and called us when he found a hand. It's Doug Langlois, used to be on the force. Now retired. He called us immediately and made sure nobody else contaminated the scene.'

'We got any outstanding MisPers?' Winter asked.

'A teenager, disappeared from Greenfields yesterday, but no other missing female reports.'

'And you're not thinking this is them?'

'No. Too much decomposition, plus we've found a wedding ring. The forensic team are saying a middle aged to elderly woman.'

Winter had reached the edge of the burial chamber stones and peered over the top at the activity going on inside. There were two white-coveralled forensics officers, and the bent shape of Dr Imran Chaudhry, their pathologist, who was examining what had been exposed so far of the body. Winter could smell the reason they were all there and instinctively brought the back of his hand to his nostrils.

'Afternoon, Dr Chaudhry,' Winter said to the stooped figure.

'DI Labey, good of you to join us,' Dr Chaudhry joked as he stood back up and turned to look up at him. 'Tear you away from your Sunday roast, did we?'

'As a matter of fact, yes,' Winter replied.

'Well, unless you want to be reacquainted with it, I'd suggest you don't come down here too close.' Dr Chaudhry raised his eyebrows.

Winter had already come to that conclusion.

'Anything you can tell me?'

'Female. From the clothes and what I'm seeing, probably fifty-five to seventy, maybe older. She wasn't frail, but also wasn't in the bloom of youth.'

'Any indications how she got here?'

'Nope. Other than I can tell you she didn't walk.'

'How badly decomposed? Are we going to be able to make up a photofit to appeal to the public for an ID?'

'You'll have a bit of a problem with that,' Dr Chaudhry replied, his eyes shifting back towards the ground in the middle of the ancient stones. 'We don't have a head.'

TWO

MONDAY

Saskia Monet sat in silence, the only noise in the room the sounds of the man in front of her breathing. It was shallow and rasping. She didn't need to look at his face to know he was angry. She could almost smell the adrenaline coming through his pores. Outside, the wind was picking up off the sea, blowing across the window in its lonely search for a home it would never find.

Saskia was a hair's breadth away from calling for assistance. She'd never once had to use her panic button since coming to La Moye prison as their chief forensic psychologist, but her hand hovered near the comforting shape of the radio inside her pocket. She kept her face impassive, but Saskia knew her own breath was shallow. Every muscle in her body on high alert.

She'd had sessions with Richard before, and there'd been no indications of this behaviour. Something had upset him, or somebody had wound him up. Question was, would he tell her what it was or was he planning on taking it out on her because he thought she was an easy target?

When the silence didn't help calm him, Saskia spoke gently

and quietly. 'Are you OK, Richard? I'm concerned about you. You don't seem your usual self.'

He looked up at her then. The pupils of his eyes dilated, an indication of his heightened emotional state. She could see his jaw tightening beneath the dark brown stubble as he ground his teeth.

Saskia knew better than to smile, even if it was a naturally reassuring thing to do. When someone was in a potentially psychotic state, they could interpret a smile as her laughing at them. She'd made that mistake once when she was younger, but not in her role as a prison psychologist.

She'd just turned seven when her psychopathic father had been on one of his rants at her mother. Saskia tried to calm the situation by disarming him with a sweet smile. She wasn't fast enough to avoid the hard slap around her head, sending her flying. 'Don't laugh at me. You think this is funny? I'll show you funny.' She could still remember her father's words as he came after her, but he was thankfully drunk and she was small and nimble. She'd scrambled off the floor and run out the house. He'd followed.

She'd been grateful that it had taken the attention off her mother, and even more grateful to have bumped into Mr and Mrs Letherington from across the street as they were arriving back from a supermarket shop. He was a big man, a former boxer, and although past his prime, Mr Letherington had drawn himself up to his full height, putting himself between her and her dad. Thankfully her father had seen sense and just sworn at her, and him, before stumbling back off to the pub where he downed a few more pints until he was too inebriated to be a danger to anyone but himself. It didn't always end like that. A year later, the Letheringtons were called as witnesses of her father's behaviour at his trial. But the trail of murdered women he'd left behind had been more than enough to convict him as the psychopathic nightingale killer.

Those years living with him had taught her more than any university degree could have done in terms of dealing with dangerous individuals. Survival was a much bigger motivator than grades.

'I know why I'm here,' Richard suddenly said.

'OK...' Saskia replied. 'Do you want to tell me why you think it is?'

'You want to get me locked away for good. Stick one of those mental labels on me. Say I shouldn't be released. Ever.'

'That's not true, Richard. I absolutely promise you that my motivation is to help you by enabling your understanding of why you're here and how you can prevent what you did from happening again. I want to see you released and not coming back.'

He stared at her intently.

'That's not what I was told.'

'Told? You know that people say things in here to cause trouble and wind you up. People get bored and your fellow prisoners don't always have your best interests as their motive.'

'It wasn't a prisoner.'

Saskia's stomach churned.

'A guard said that to you?'

'I ain't grassing anyone up.' Richard narrowed his eyes. 'How do I know you're telling me the truth.'

'Do you want to read the notes I've written from our last two sessions?' Saskia offered. 'I promise you that I'm only here to help you, Richard.' She could see the immediate threat had passed; just the act of having the conversation and thinking about what she was saying had helped Richard calm down a little, so she tried something else. 'If you thought I was trying to trick you, then why did you come along to the session?'

'I only heard on the way over,' Richard replied, failing to realise he'd just given her the name of the guard who'd told him. Saskia wasn't in the least surprised. Mark Byrne had delivered him to the session and she knew that Mark definitely didn't like her.

She changed the subject, moving him onto firmer, calmer ground. 'Why don't we talk about the art classes you've been doing?'

Richard's face immediately broke into a smile. 'Yeah, really enjoying them. Never thought I had it in me.'

Saskia didn't mention the fact that painting was obviously something he connected with, if the state of the shop that he'd robbed had been anything to go by. He'd daubed paint across the walls and windows like some huge abstract expressionist art installation. Unfortunately for him, he'd been concentrating so hard on the artwork, he failed to leave the building before the police arrived. It hadn't been his first offence and so a custodial sentence was meted out. Saskia had suggested the art classes as a way for him to express himself. Some of his work had been really promising, along with being thankfully within the law.

'The teacher thinks you're doing really well. I saw the still life you did. It was pretty amazing.'

'You think?' Richard's face lit up like a child being praised, then clouded over again. 'Or you just saying that?'

'I mean it. I'm really pleased you have found something you enjoy. How does it make you feel when you're painting?'

'Like I'm not me. Like I'm free,' Richard replied, relaxing back into his chair, the final tension of earlier dissipating. 'I don't mean free from here; I mean free, free. You know, like I'm soaring above everything.' He stopped. 'Does that sound sad?'

'Absolutely not, that's fantastic. I feel like that when I'm surfing. We all need to find something that makes us feel good; that can give us an outlet for our emotions, stress, and our anger.'

Saskia knew that Richard's childhood had been spent with an abusive father and a mother who prioritised her drug habit and not him. Like so many young people who experienced childhood trauma, it had led to behavioural, emotional, and social disorders. Research showed this complex PTSD or trauma has a profound impact on brain development and stress, leading to lifelong issues. Schooling was inevitably one of the first to suffer. Richard had left compulsory education with barely a qualification to his name and had drifted into crime as an easy option for making ends meet. When Saskia met people like Richard, she felt eternally grateful that her own resilience meant she hadn't followed the same path. There'd been some hiccups along the way, but she put her survival down to having to look out for her brother which meant she could externalise a lot of her own fears and trauma. Her hope for Richard, was that they'd get him onto a programme which would give him a means to make his living and that he'd find a new route in life, some self-esteem, and another way of expressing his frustrations other than illegally painting other people's property. These sessions were to help him to understand why he'd ended up in La Moye and how he could help himself to stay out of there.

By the time Richard went back to his cell block, he and Saskia were chatting happily about art and its different forms and whether some of the modern art you saw nowadays was really art for everyone to enjoy, or just the creator being selfish.

It wasn't Mark Byrne who came to take him back, much to Saskia's relief. She needed to process this latest escalation in Byrne's behaviour towards her. Of all the people in La Moye, he was the one she was most wary of. A psychopath on the wrong side of the bars. What he'd done today could have potentially resulted in her being injured, perhaps killed, and Richard having his life further ruined for no reason. She had to think about how she was going to deal with Mark Byrne, because ignoring him and his behaviour was clearly not working.

Saskia looked at her mobile phone once Richard had gone. She had a missed call and the name that came up on the screen gave her heart an instant buzz of excitement. DI Winter Labey was a man she loved spending time with. In fact, she'd spend a lot more time with him if she could, only the predicament her brother, David, put her in meant she had to keep him at arm's length. It didn't stop the longing though, and they'd not seen each other for a couple of weeks.

Saskia had helped Winter on a couple of cases in the summer, and they'd bumped into each other a few times since at St Ouen, both of them keen surfers; but with autumn arriving, the weather had connived to keep them apart. That had probably been a good thing as each time she saw him, she'd felt her resolve to not get involved with him dissolving like the sea salt.

Now, as she dialled his number, she felt the familiar butterflies and wished that life was simpler.

'Saskia,' Winter greeted her. He sounded as though he was outside and walking. There was wind against the mouthpiece and his breath juddered with his footsteps. 'Thanks for calling back. I've got a bit of a puzzle for you, wondered if you might be able to help us on another case?'

'Not the body in the dolmen, is it?' she said, remembering the story on the local TV news last night.

'It is, but it's not quite as straightforward as that I'm afraid.'

'They never are.'

Winter sighed. 'No. Are you able to meet up to go through what we have?'

'Sure.' The prospect of seeing Winter and spending time with him didn't need any persuasion.

'Great. Would you be able to come to the station first and then we can do the site visits – and how about after I buy you dinner? So we can discuss it.' Winter added the last part quickly. He clearly didn't want her getting the wrong impression.

Saskia wished he felt the same way as she did and that her brother, David, was just like everyone else's brother.

THREE

The doctor handed David a mirror so he could study every centimetre of his face.

'So the Botox has settled in nicely,' she said to him, showing him a polaroid of his face prior to any injections. At just thirty-three, the evidence of ageing was minimal, but he'd noticed it.

David inspected her handiwork around his eyes and on his forehead, where not a wrinkle could be seen.

'What about my mouth,' he said to her, pursing his lips at the reflection of himself.

'I think a little bit of filler and some hyaluronic acid will sort that out.' Her face was professional, but her eyes danced at him.

David tore his eyes away from his own reflection to look at the doctor. She was about ten years older than him but you'd never have guessed it. Her skin was flawless and he'd seen her in the gym so knew that the perfect body shape was achieved through hard work. Today she had on a short skirt and a blouse, which he'd swear had had one extra button done up when she'd said goodbye to her last patient. If he didn't know better, this woman was trying to hit on him.

'OK,' he said to her, giving what he deemed to be one of his best smiles – the teeth had cost him a fortune too. 'Let's do it.'

'Great, I'll schedule you in for the treatment,' she replied, turning back round to her laptop on the side and allowing David to return his gaze to his own reflection.

The doctor bent forward onto the countertop, leaning her elbows on the surface and allowing her skirt to ride a little higher up the back of her legs.

'How about the fifteenth, does that work for you?' she asked.

He looked around the mirror. She was positively thrusting her arse towards him.

He assessed the view before checking his mobile calendar.

'Sure, what time on the fifteenth?'

She was there for his taking.

'Do you want to do last thing, so it doesn't interrupt work? Say, five p.m.?'

'Yes. In the diary,' he said, typing it in and closing the app.

The complication was that his girlfriend, Jackie, was also one of her patients, and the doctor was fully aware of their relationship. The danger was that she wasn't married. Single women had nothing to lose. If she was this desperate for him now, she might cause him some trouble down the line.

A couple of years ago, David would have jumped straight in and not given any thought to potential consequences. Why shouldn't he just do what he wanted? But years of sessions with his sister, Saskia, meant he was now able to weigh up if a decision was going to be good for him, or not, in the long term. Issues, like the doctor could create, might prevent him from reaching his ultimate goals. A quick fuck would be moderately enjoyable, but it was like an apex predator snacking on an insect. There was very little challenge to give him a real thrill. He had far bigger fish to fry, like ensuring that the house he currently lived in became his. For that, he needed to not raise any suspicions from Jackie. He had a plan, and any illicit love affairs had to be kept quiet. Jackie wouldn't tolerate infidelity and he wanted to sort her out his own way. The quick remedial action he'd taken to get rid of Allan was enjoyable and necessary, but what he had planned for Jackie would bring more prolonged pleasure.

David swung his legs off the couch and walked up behind the doctor so they were just centimetres away from each other. He could almost feel the blood pumping fast around her body as she willed him to take her.

'Pretty necklace,' he said, looking down at her cleavage where a small diamond-encrusted cross sat nestling in the Y of her breasts. 'May I?' he asked, enjoying the thrill of teasing her.

'Yes,' she replied a little breathlessly. Not her usual professional voice.

He allowed his fingers to gently brush over the top of her breasts as he lifted the cross from her skin and looked at it. He heard her catch her breath as he looked up.

'Very nice,' he said as he let the necklace drop back down. He looked into her eyes, her face just inches from his own. 'I'll see you on the fifteenth then,' he said to her, and turned and walked out of the consulting room.

That had been more fun than just giving her what she wanted.

David's thoughts turned back to Jackie. He'd already begun the next phase of his plan. Last night they'd gone out with friends for dinner and he'd arranged it so that the time in her phone calendar was half an hour later than it had been originally. Arriving late had flustered her, and the friends witnessed him telling her gently that he'd thought she'd originally said seven, not seven thirty. When she'd gone to the toilet, he'd excused her forgetfulness.

'She's not quite herself lately. I know she's worried about inheriting her mother's dementia. But I'm sure she's fine, just too much on at work maybe,' he'd said compassionately.

They'd looked at one another and then agreed with him.

He'd started to plant his seeds.

FOUR

Saskia drove her car to the police station in St Helier. The cold rain that had whipped up from nowhere, and was now sheeting down across her windscreen, had prompted her to choose a warmer and drier option than her motorbike.

The morning had begun with the promise of sunshine but hadn't taken long to change its mind. Tomorrow came with the promise of heavy mist or fog which could smother the island and lose it to the world, preventing the planes from landing and boats leaving. Bizarrely, she loved that about the place, giving it an almost secret hideaway feel – as though the world and all its troubles couldn't touch them here. Jersey rarely saw snow, or dropped much below freezing, and certainly was warmer and sunnier than almost anywhere else in the British Isles, but it still experienced the raw power of nature's climate. Out on the west coast was the most exposed to the weather fronts coming off the Atlantic and funnelling down the English Channel. As she drove into St Helier, the rain began to ease and Saskia was relieved to find it had almost stopped by the time she'd parked her car and started walking to the police station off the roundabout.

Winter came down to the reception to meet her and let her in through the secure door of the modern building.

It was ridiculous but she felt nervous seeing him. These were feelings she'd never felt before. The usual teenage crushes had bypassed her life, frightened away by her brother and their family's reputation. It was only once she'd changed her name and moved to another town, that people began to look at her as human again. All great experience for understanding the prisoners she worked with, just not so great for forging long-term personal relationships. She'd long since shut that door.

'How's things?' Winter asked, holding the security door open for her.

'The usual, not managed to get out on the surf for a couple of weeks though.' Her voice seemed to her to come out forced.

'Thought I hadn't seen you. I went last week but it was messy, we didn't stay in for long. Doubt I'm going to get the chance now for at least the next week or so.'

'I take it this case is the one reported in the local news? A body found at a dolmen in St Clement?'

'It is, but they don't know the half of it. I suspect more will get out over the next twenty-four hours, but basically we're dealing with multiple sites. I don't think this is some domestic that's gone nuclear, hence why I've called you.'

Saskia's mind ran through what she'd read and heard in the local media over the last twelve hours. It was sketchy, just that a body of a woman had been found buried in the dolmen site at Mont Ubé.

'Who was she? The woman at Mont Ubé?'

'Well, that's part of our problem. We've no idea.'

'You think she's from off island?'

'Not necessarily, although it's possible. It's just we literally only have a body. No ID and more critically no head. Well, actually, technically that's not totally true. We've just found a head, but we don't think it's hers.' Winter frowned at Saskia as they walked into the main office. 'I'll fill you in,' he added.

Walking into Winter's office was a bit like returning home. Saskia recognised most of the faces, although she was relieved to see no sign of Detective Chief Inspector Christopher Sharpe. She'd disagreed with his take on the last two cases, as had Winter, and she wasn't yet ready to be bombarded by his opinions on this one.

She raised her hand and smiled at Jonno – Detective Sergeant Jonathon Vibert – who was not only a good detective, but also Winter's childhood friend. He beamed back at her, always welcoming and chilled. The curly hair of Detective Constable Pete Edwards was also bobbed her way, and DC Sarah Fuller gave her a friendly 'hi' as she passed by her desk.

Winter pulled up a chair for Saskia and sat down at his computer.

'Sorry, did you want a drink or anything before we start?'

'No, you're OK,' she replied. He was clearly eager to crack on and so was she.

'Right, so as you've heard, a body was found at Mont Ubé.' He clicked up some images on the screen. Photographs of the gravesite in various stages of exhumation showed a shallow hole in which the shape of a woman's body could be easily seen. 'We're just waiting on the full post-mortem report and it's going to take us a few days to get more details on tests, but looks to be an older woman, fifty-five plus, although Dr Chaudhry is thinking more like sixty-five to seventy. Difficult to know cause of death due to the decapitation, but when we go on to the next disposition site, you'll see that we're thinking possible strangulation.'

'So the killer strangled her and then decapitated her?'

'That's looking most likely at this stage. This Jane Doe has been dead around two weeks, but she hasn't been in the ground that long. Notice he hasn't wrapped her in anything. We are asking the public to help us as to when the ground was disturbed – at the moment we have the original report from a member of the public and that was three days ago. There's a house behind the dolmen, but they hadn't noticed any unusual activity there.'

Saskia strained to see the details of the muddied corpse.

'Is she lying curled up, or on her back?'

'She was lying on her back but her lower legs were bent back. We think that could be simply because he didn't dig a big enough hole, as he's damaged the knees to make her legs fold sufficiently.'

'Anything put in with her?'

Winter shook his head. 'Her hands were folded across her body.'

Saskia felt Winter's eyes on her face; she turned and looked at him, giving a slight nod to say she was ready for him to continue.

'So, realising we were missing a head, we checked all the other dolmen sites in the island and found two other disposition sites.'

'Le Couperon.' Winter brought up the images of another dolmen, this time with covering capstones on the uprights. 'Another woman's body, minus its head found at this site, but this one had been there longer. We think maybe because it would have been buried in the summer and the earth dried out quickly by the sun, people didn't notice it so much. Again, a woman of fifty-five plus. Dr Chaudhry is looking at her in more detail today with an expert from the UK. She'd been there about two or three months so she's not in a particularly good state. He buried her deeper.'

'Two or three months? So why is nobody reporting these women missing, or do you have outstanding MisPer cases?'

'Good question and no. We have two men and a teenager currently registered as missing, but no women.'

'So they could still be from off-island, or perhaps tourists?'

'It's possible. But, our third disposition site, La Pouquelaye de Faldouët, gave us at least some answers. In there, we found a head. We're not yet sure who the head belongs to, or even if it belongs to either of our Jane Does, because she was put in the ground around a month ago, so in between the other two burials.'

Saskia let out a big thoughtful sigh and leant back in her chair.

'Are there any indications that the two women are from the same family?'

Winter shook his head. 'Not that we can say so far, but obviously all the DNA and test results are ongoing.'

'Any other damage to the bodies besides the heads? I mean were there indications of sexual assault or other wounds and marks?'

'Not with our first Jane Doe. The second one, I'm not sure we're going to be able to ascertain if she was sexually assaulted, but I'm waiting on Dr Chaudhry and his UK colleagues to give us more on her. I'm going to go out publicly with their clothing, see if anyone recognises that. If they do live locally, then somebody must have noticed they've not been around.'

'You'd think so, wouldn't you? And these are disposition sites, so somewhere we have the original crime scenes,' Saskia thought aloud.

'Yup.'

'Interesting that they're all east of the island, so a big geographical clue as to where our killer is likely to be based.'

'Looks that way, unless they're super smart and are bluffing us.'

'Or there's some other reason why the east is required, such as a pagan ritual in need of sunrise.'

Saskia looked towards the window. The sky had cleared and

a pale winter blue canopy looked back at her. 'Is it too late to visit the sites now, do you think?'

'No, we can go now. I'll bring a torch in case it starts to get dark. But I reckon we've got about two hours, then I'll buy you that dinner I promised you.'

Saskia wished he hadn't reminded her about that; her ridiculous nerves instantly returned. The prospect of sitting across a table from Winter and only being able to focus on him – and vice versa – was far more nerve-wracking than sitting in a room with a bunch of convicted killers.

The huge elephant in their relationship was David, and most particularly, whatever role he'd played in the death of Allan Hall. Her brother had repeatedly denied having any involvement in his murder, kept insisting that it had been Allan's boyfriend, Kevin. But that didn't explain why he'd brought round Jackie's stolen necklace for Saskia to look after a couple of days before Allan went missing.

'I found it in the garage. I was looking for some screen wash, and there it was, tucked away hidden at the back of a shelf.'

'So why didn't you tell Jackie and put it back?' Saskia had questioned.

'OK, I'll admit that I thought it could be a bit of a backup plan in case I needed it. If Allan or Kevin had stolen it, then it was their fault. They stole it from Jackie. I just took it off them. I might need to leave one day and that's my little emergency nest egg. Jackie could dump me at any time and then where would I be?'

The thought was a feasible one for David's selfish personality, but was that all?

'It could be why Kevin killed Allan, maybe he thought he'd been double crossed,' she had pressed.

David had just shrugged his shoulders.

'You told me you'd bought it for Jackie's birthday. You lied to me.'

'You wouldn't have looked after it otherwise.'

'You need to give it back,' Saskia had insisted. *'You could put it somewhere in the garage again, and then just happen to find it.'*

'No.' David's face had hardened. *'It's gone. The insurance has already paid Jackie. She can go buy another one. It's just a necklace.'*

And that had been the end of it. He wouldn't discuss it anymore. The only comfort that Saskia took was that the police charged Kevin for Allan's murder, so they must have had evidence, and at least David was telling the truth about that – and if he was, then he might be telling the truth about the necklace. Her worst nightmare was that it had been David who had killed Allan. While she didn't like the idea that he'd taken the necklace, it didn't look as though he'd been the one to steal it originally or physically hurt anybody, and that was the main thing.

For a couple of weeks, Saskia had struggled to not tell Winter the truth, not to just come out with it and free herself of the burden. If she came clean about having a brother and who he was, then she wouldn't have to hide things from him. Perhaps she could even secretly return the necklace herself and Jackie would find it?

She didn't do either. Returning the necklace would anger her brother and while he might be stable now, it would break the trust between them. Without their regular contact, David risked succumbing to more extreme behaviour. That could result in someone being hurt, him being imprisoned, and she doubted Winter would consider her as suitable girlfriend material then. Instead, as time went on, the idea of just keeping quiet became more acceptable and she learnt to live with it. Just like she'd learnt to live with all the other secrets in her family. Survival on the best terms she could get.

One advantage of working with convicted criminals was

that you got to learn what mistakes they'd made and how the police had caught them. Saskia took the necklace from where she'd hidden it in her house, and buried it. Not in the garden where ground penetrating radar might see the disturbed earth, but someplace else where nobody would ever think to look. Going forward she would be keeping an even closer eye on David. She had limits to her loyalty and she'd sworn that never again would she cover for him if he hurt somebody. She knew what he was, what he was capable of – and what she too was capable of doing.

FIVE

Winter had forgotten just how much he enjoyed being in Saskia's company. Well, not exactly forgotten; he'd tried to deny the feelings, telling himself they clearly weren't reciprocated and he couldn't ruin a professional relationship. Seeing her again after a break of a couple of weeks relit all the fires.

They'd started off at the nearest dolmen on Mont Ubé. The area was still cordoned off to the public, although there was little they expected to get from any further forensic analysis. The Société had been concerned about too many people turning up and disturbing the site in order to see where the gory burial had been.

When they visited scenes like this, Winter knew to leave Saskia to concentrate and get a feel for the place. She wasn't a woman who was slow in coming forward: if she wanted to ask him something, she would.

'Where does that path lead?' she said to him after a couple of minutes, narrowing her eyes and looking off down the clearly trodden footpath which wound its way through small trees and bushes.

'The woods lead into a small agricultural field and then

beyond that is where Nicolle Tower stands. There are footpaths through there and you can even drive a car into that field up the entrance drive, but it's for the holiday let only.'

'Holiday let?'

'Sorry, yeah, the tower is rented out by the Landmark Trust. It was originally some kind of folly, then modified and used by the Germans as an observation tower during the occupation. It's been renovated so people can stay there. We're in contact with the Landmark Trust, trying to find out who was there at the time we think our Jane Doe was interred.'

'So that couldn't be the murder site?'

'No. We've accessed the tower. Nothing to indicate anything took place there.'

'So if they came that way they'd have had to come past that tower to get here?'

'Yes. But you can also come up through the woods to the left there. It's a steep slope, a bit like the one we just climbed up from La Blinerie but a bit harder going and more trip hazards. That's going to be fairly tough if you're carrying a dead weight.'

'Doable for someone who is fit?'

'She wasn't a big woman, in height or build, and your head is about eight per cent of your average body weight, so you can take around ten pounds off for that. I'd say it was doable but he would need to be fairly strong.'

'If he came the same way as us, he'd have had to park at the bottom on the road like we just did.'

'Yup but that area of the road is dark, if he came late at night there'd have probably been other cars there too and so it's unlikely that anyone would particularly notice or think that unusual. We've got no CCTV around the area and door to doors haven't led to any leads.'

'This house doesn't have any handy cameras in its back garden then?' Saskia asked nodding towards the cream-coloured house that stood around thirty yards away.

'Security lights, but unfortunately no cameras. They didn't see or hear anything in the last few weeks that made them think someone was up to no good at the dolmen.'

'In the dark down in the grave pit, it would be hard to see someone, and you're unlikely to be disturbed up here at night.'

'Agreed.'

'And no other signs that anything has been disturbed, nothing left behind or written on the stones?'

Winter shook his head.

'OK, ready for the next one.'

Winter drove just over fifteen minutes away to a field above the picturesque harbour of Gorey.

'Nice round here,' Saskia commented as they got out of the car and looked at the picture-perfect houses and green fields. The sea and the coast of France were also clearly visible across the fields, the continent of Europe a hazy line along the top of the blue water.

'Yeah, wasn't so nice about a decade ago when the children's home was being investigated and excavated.'

'I read about that.' Saskia looked around her, as though expecting to still see the scenes that had been on the TV and in the newspapers.

'Yup, that's another story for another day. The dolmen is along the road and in a field.'

They walked up some steps past the sign which told of the Dolmen's history and the remains that were found when the earth mound was excavated.

'Amazing to think this neolithic grave has been here six thousand years,' Saskia exclaimed in front of him. She stopped at the start of a long run of upright stones, around three feet or so in height. A greyer granite than the previous dolmen at Mont Ubé, with some appearing as though they'd been whitewashed, the white lichen had covered them so thickly. They led to what looked like a stone lean-to of several uprights holding a large flat capstone on top, which Winter had read on the sign weighed twenty-four tons.

'The head was buried under the capstone covered area there.' Winter pointed to an area of bare earth at the back of the covered chamber. 'There's not usually any grass growing there so it wasn't so noticeable.'

'This ground would have been hard to dig,' Saskia said to him, scanning the earth. 'There's lots of stones and pieces of granite, and it's hard and well trodden.'

'I agree. Most of the dolmen sites are like that and again shows the killer was fit.'

'And had a really strong commitment to bury the head and bodies at these sites. There are a million other ways he could have disposed of them which would have been one heck of a lot easier.'

'Any thoughts yet on why that would be?' Winter tried his luck.

'Not yet. I need to know more about the women first. I'd guess this place is pitch dark at night and nobody's likely to wander in, so again he'd have managed to do what he needed without anyone seeing.'

'We did speak to one neighbour who said they thought they'd heard something over here a month or so back, in the early hours of the morning. We've asked them to try to remember which day it was and they were going to check their diaries see if they could work it out.'

'What are the generally known thoughts about these dolmens? Do people see them as graves or something else?'

'I think most islanders think of them as graves where important people would have been buried, a bit like the barrows or burial mounds in the UK, although actually Doug, who found our first Jane Doe and is a keen archaeologist, says that the thinking now is they were more like celebration and focus sites for the community. You'll notice they're on prominent sites. People might have come here to worship and give thanks, perhaps make sacrifices. We know that La Hougue Bie, the biggest site in the island, was positioned for the solstice. Having said that, they did find human remains here, so at some point people were buried, but not necessarily like we would bury people in graves today. I think they often burnt them and broke the bodies up, if I remember rightly.'

'But our Jane Doe was placed in the traditional Christian style?'

'On her back yes, but minus her head.'

'Sometimes bodies are decapitated for spiritual reasons. You know, the killer might think they're witches or vampires, or simply wants to stop them from ever being able to be resurrected, if he believes in the old Christian teachings. We need to know more about how he's treated their bodies to begin to understand his motivation for bringing them to the dolmens.'

'I don't understand, like you said, why he went to so much trouble to bury them here. I sure wouldn't want to try to dig a grave in this ground.'

'It's possibly a respect thing. He could be torn. But like I say, I need to know more about the state of the bodies first.' Saskia walked off around the back of the capstone. 'You didn't find any symbols or other objects at any of the sites, did you?'

'Nope. Nothing. Of course it's possible that someone else removed them, and again we are appealing for any information from the public on that, but there was certainly nothing by the time we got here.'

Saskia reappeared round the other side of the capstone, her brow furrowed in concentration. Winter watched her until he realised he might be staring and forced himself to look away. The sky was beginning to colour, the sun now far out west.

'We'd better get to the third site before it starts getting dark,' he said to her.

'Yes. Ready.'

The third site was Le Dolmen du Couperon, which they got to via a narrow winding road down a steep hill.

'This the only way to go?' Saskia had asked him on the way.

'It is by car, and a right pain if you meet someone going the other way. It's a lovely spot though.'

They arrived at a tiny gravel car park with footpaths leading off in various directions, and a clear entrance to the dolmen, opposite the sea.

'They certainly chose nice spots for these places,' she mused, looking around her.

'It's stunning here, isn't it? Views across the sea, that little bay down there to the right and there's also walks through that wooded area and along the coastline. It's so peaceful even today, so you can imagine how idyllic it was back then. Also seen its fair share of war due to its location.'

'Here?'

'Yes there's a battery on the headland above. Don't forget the French weren't always our friends, long before the Germans invaded.'

He led her into the site where the dolmen sat and they were immediately faced with a small stone and brick building.

'That's a guardhouse, built in the 1600s to support the battery. If you can imagine this place without the trees and shrubs we have now, you can see how both the dolmen and the guardhouse would have had uninterrupted views.'

'Is there anything that links the three dolmens we've been to besides the fact they're in the east?'

'I don't think so, other than that they're ancient graves. This one is the youngest of the three, only about five thousand years old. It was also almost certainly our first disposition site.'

'Secluded, especially at night, but at all three he risked being found, and here he'd have struggled to get away. He would have had to bring her in the car. No way he'd have been able to carry a body the distance otherwise.'

'Yes, unless he's someone you wouldn't suspect. Someone you'd expect to see here.'

Saskia wandered around the burial site, thinking and studying the area.

'The current view in the team is that this could be related to some kind of pagan beliefs, or even witchcraft.'

'Why witchcraft? Was there anything that suggested that?'

'No, just the locations and it's always more disturbing when the heads have been taken.'

'I think we're more likely to discover that it's either someone with a mental illness, or a psychopath. There's no signs of a ritual having taken place.'

Winter nodded slowly in agreement. Dusk was falling fast, the east side of the island having lost the sun to the west, and shadows were growing longer.

'This place gets a lot more creepy in the evening with the shadows,' Winter voiced aloud.

'That's a good point, this spot is perfectly placed for sunrise. You should check when the solstice and equinox dates were and see if they coincide with the internments. That would be a big clue if it was someone following some kind of pagan religion.'

'Will do. I'm hoping Dr Chaudhry will have some information for me later today or tomorrow. Shall we go get that dinner?'

'Sure,' Saskia replied.

Winter wondered if she found the thought of staying in the dark with the ancient grave more appealing than dinner with him; she certainly didn't look or sound enthused.

'If you'd rather not tonight, then that's not a problem,' he said to her, 'it was only a suggestion.'

'Oh no, that will be lovely, thank you. If you want to...'

Winter thought that for a woman who was so insightful about psychology and how people thought and behaved, she was clearly missing just how much he really wanted to spend time in her company. Perhaps that was a good thing considering she was obviously not interested in him.

SIX

She'd started again.

'You always were a useless lump of lard; if only your father could see you now. After all I've done for you, given up my life to care for you, this is how you repay me?'

'I'm sorry, it was an accident.'

'Clumsy, that's what you are. A clumsy idiot.'

He had quickly soaked up as much of the spilt soup as he could, before getting a damp cloth and wiping away the residue. It had only been chicken and sweetcorn, so thankfully no dark or bright food colours to stain the carpet.

She sat spooning the rest of the soup into her mouth, watching him. The disgust and disdain on her face clear to see.

He could feel her eyes drilling into his skull, burning into his brain. Watching his every move.

By the time he'd finished, so had she.

'I'm done,' she'd announced, instantly expecting him to pick up her bowl and spoon and take them to the kitchen. She kept her tray, ready for the main course. He hoped that didn't end up on the floor. It had been his old slipper which made him trip. The sole was coming away on the bottom and so he'd caught it on the carpet. He'd get some glue tomorrow to fix it. In the meantime, he'd be ultra-careful to make sure her lasagne didn't end up on the floor too.

When he walked back into the sitting room, she watched his every move, making him self-conscious of each step he took. He held his breath until he'd placed the plate on her tray and she'd started tucking into it. There was never a thank you.

She wasn't interested in his company; *Coronation Street* was far more of a draw, and so he'd taken his lasagne down to his shed. His safe place. She couldn't come down here: he made sure to keep the garden wild at the bottom and the path uneven. Her mobility was just about gone as it was; she'd barely ventured out into the garden at all in the last two years.

Just in case, and to make sure nobody else entered, he kept it locked. There were two padlocks on the door and he'd fitted metal grills to the windows so that someone couldn't enter that way. You could never be too sure nowadays with all the drug addicts around. Opportune thieves liked garden equipment. Not that he had any, but they didn't know that.

This was where he met his friends, his hangout. Nobody was allowed in here without his say so.

He removed the keys from around his thick neck, the chain brushing against his beard, and used them to spring the padlocks open, placing his dinner on the ground so he could use both hands to take off the thick chain and open the door. He breathed in the familiar smell, his homecoming, and sighed with relief.

As he switched on the light, the faces of his friends were illuminated, all looking at him with respect and love. Some of them had glass eyes, some didn't have any eyes at all as such, but he knew they saw him all the same. And they kept a watch on *her* too. His friends made sure that she did as she was told.

She watched him again as he walked across to the chair

with his dinner. But he didn't feel so self-conscious this time. This time he was in control and she had to do what he said.

The shed was carpeted and the windows curtained. He had a fridge and a freezer, along with a kettle and two mugs that he'd not been allowed to have in the house.

He sat down next to her and turned the TV on, making a point of moving through the channels so she saw her beloved *Coronation Street* for just a slither of a glimpse before he changed channel. That brought a small smile to his lips.

Then he settled to watch the *Motorway Cops*, which he knew she hated, and began eating his dinner.

She could say nothing. Eat nothing. No insults. No demands. No put downs. No way to make him feel inferior. He'd sewn her lips together to be sure of her silence.

He was in control now.

SEVEN

Maybe it was the warm restaurant after the chill fresh air outside. Maybe she was tired. Maybe it was because their dinner orders seemed to be taking forever to come. Or perhaps it was the wine that Winter kept insisting on pouring in her glass, but Saskia felt a little tipsy.

'Sorry about this, they're usually really good here,' Winter apologised to her. 'All the restaurants are struggling to get the staff at the moment.'

'It's fine, but I really can't drink anymore as I've got to drive home when we get back to St Helier and I'm pretty sure I've already had my quota, officer.'

Winter smirked at her humour.

'I'll drive you home, don't worry. It's the least I can do after all your help. I'll also pick you up again tomorrow for our breakfast visit to Dr Chaudhry and then you can get your car after.'

Dr Chaudhry had called Winter half an hour ago and said he was ready to go through preliminary findings with him. They'd agreed to meet in the morning, and Saskia said she'd like to be there to hear what he had to say. While she didn't relish the idea of spending her early morning in a mortuary examination room with two rotting corpses and a head, it was going to be critical for her assessment of who had killed the two women, and that was far more important than her own comfort.

Talking of comfort, sitting directly in front of a man she was extremely attracted to but couldn't touch was making her feel decidedly uncomfortable. She resisted Winter's offer of driving her home initially, but the glass of wine became harder to ignore. She sipped it to alleviate her nerves, but then discovered the bottom of the glass.

Winter had been talking about dolmens and Jersey's neolithic history, which was really interesting, but she had found herself watching his mouth and wishing she could kiss it instead of concentrating on what he was saying. Not for the first time, she wished that her family situation was different. Winter was a handsome man in a rugged sporty way, well built, with a healthy tan, and you could almost smell the fresh air and exercise coming off him. Saskia loved surfing just as much as he did, and they'd found a congenial co-existence together on the waves.

'Do you think we're dealing with a psychopath?' Winter suddenly asked her, bringing her back to the conversation and not her hormones.

'Possibly, but equally it could be somebody who has an extreme mental illness. At this stage, I would err towards the latter, just because a psychopath doesn't care about consequence, so why go to all that trouble burying them like that? We need to work out why he's taken them to the dolmen sites. Is it because he recognises that what he's done is wrong and although he can't bury them in a formal churchyard, he's doing the best he thinks he can for them? In which case I think it's unlikely he's a psychopath. They don't have any regard for rules and societal norms, or their victims, they just do what they want. On the other hand, someone with a mental illness could be emotionally driven with deep-seated anxiety and insecurities. Plus they have the opportunity for remorse, which a psychopath doesn't.'

'How do you work with psychopaths? I mean they must be one of the most feared and hated sections of the population. I've met a couple in my time, and I just can't get my head around their complete lack of emotion or morality. Isn't that incredibly hard for you in your job?'

Saskia felt her stomach squirm at his words. If he knew about her family, about the blood that ran through her veins, he wouldn't be sitting here with her now. He would despise her too. She swallowed hard and carried on, like she always had. 'You know, in some ways, once you get what they're about, it's a whole lot easier to deal with them than you think because although they'd hate for me to say this, they're actually quite black and white; unlike most of us who are moral quagmires and a whole smorgasbord of irrational emotional motivations. You and I are no more important to them as living creatures than the chairs we're sitting on. It's that simple. Everything is about them and what they're getting out of a situation. Once you get that about them, they become easier to deal with.'

Winter raised his eyebrows at her, concentrating. 'Go on then, enlighten this particular quagmire of morality, would you?' He smiled as he said it.

'Well, you've probably met a lot more psychopaths than you realise,' Saskia started, 'and the first thing to understand is that there are those we call high functioning and those who are lower functioning. The high functioning psychopaths can be found in politics, the law, and at the top of businesses. They achieve because they're intelligent, while also being ruthless and confident, and have learnt to hide in plain sight by looking as though they're playing by the rules in order to get what they want. They still have a massively inflated view of their own importance, which can come across as arrogance, but some people find that an attractive trait of self-confidence. They get off on having power over others and contrary to populist media, that doesn't mean they are all killers, although admittedly a psychopath is around twice as likely to commit a violent crime as other members of the prison population. They're con men, taking what they want from people and not giving anything back; they're egocentric and driven by instant gratification without guilt. Relationships are usually impersonal and they're not the faithful type.'

'Nice people to know then. Come to think of it, I can think of a couple of high-flying execs and wealthy residents over here that would fit that bill.'

'I've no doubt you can. One per cent of the population, mostly male, are thought to be psychopaths. There are also the less intelligent and impulsive types,' Saskia continued, 'those we call lower functioning, who are more likely to have poor family backgrounds and to get caught. They tend to be more likely to lash out if insulted or annoyed, they don't have inhibitions and they don't have remorse. Although I wouldn't call it a lack of self-control, it's not like an emotional outburst with someone getting angry, because they don't do emotions, it's controlled aggression. Callous and businesslike, that's the trademark of all psychopaths. Afterwards they'll usually blame the victim for why they attacked, saying they were provoked. They also tend to be irresponsible, because after all, it's only them who they answer to and societal rules are unreasonable.'

At that point, their dinners arrived, and Saskia realised she'd been doing all the talking for the past few minutes.

'Sorry, I can tend to wax lyrical on the topic.' She gave a half smile to Winter, before thanking the waitress for bringing her dinner.

Winter also thanked the waitress. 'No please, don't apologise. I find it interesting. So how do you treat them? If someone comes into prison on a five-year sentence, how do you try to prevent them from going straight back out and doing it again once they're released, if they have no remorse?'

Saskia watched him tuck into his cod and chips dinner with relish and was taken back to a few weeks before, when he'd been in her cottage after bringing round a takeaway. She'd been so close then to succumbing to her feelings for him, and here she was again not having learnt her lesson. She dropped her gaze to the chicken Caesar salad on her own plate and forced herself to focus on his question.

'Well that's the conundrum that has preoccupied psychologists since psychopaths were first identified. How do you persuade someone who has no guilt, remorse, emotion, and fear of consequence, not to hurt others who mean nothing to them?'

Saskia looked back up at Winter's expectant face and wished that she really did have the magic bullet, that she could cure her brother and be confident he wouldn't hurt anyone ever again. Then she'd be free to live her own life too.

'Truth is most think it's impossible, but there are always new techniques and treatments being developed.'

'What do you do? How do you deal with your prisoners?'

'For those who are intelligent, it's a case of constantly reinforcing what they have to lose if they don't play by society's rules. They don't like being told what to do and be put in jail. The only persuasion tactic we have is their own self-interest, but you'll never change their nature. Although they do tend to mellow with age.'

'Hmm!' Winter replied, nodding in thought. 'So, if they don't have any emotions and fear, they should be easy to tell apart from the rest of us.'

'I wish,' Saskia joked. 'If they're smart, they not only learn how to fake psychological testing, but they also become very adept at mirroring our emotions and how we behave in order to manipulate us. That's why group therapy is a disaster, it's like a training ground for them.'

'Any expert telltale signs that someone is a psychopath?'

'There's a very detailed checklist been developed by Robert D. Hare, to help with diagnosis, but the main signs are being superficial, grandiose, having no empathy or guilt and being deceitful and manipulative, but often they're quite witty, very persuasive and charming. On the surface they can appear attractive and likeable, although they can also be seen as arrogant and cocky. Some of them are incredibly charismatic and they will always have a justification for why they did something or hurt someone. They also seek out excitement and are likely to have had early behavioural problems as children, but that could also describe some other conditions so it's not an easily cut and dried diagnosis. It does require an expert to properly identify them.'

'But it's not a mental illness, right? When people we've arrested are diagnosed as psychopaths, they don't get to go to a medical facility, they are put in the main prison system.'

'That's right, I know a lot of the public think it's a mental illness, but it's not. It's a personality disorder and their brains actually show physically different characteristics to ours when scanned. They're wired differently. Some people who have lived with psychopaths have said that there was something missing in their relationship and in their family member or friend, but they found it hard to put their finger on what it was.'

'So based on what you've seen so far of our burials, you're thinking they're not psychopathic because it looks like they've shown some care in the internments, albeit I'm sure the victims and their relatives won't agree the killer was particularly caring.'

'Yes. A psychopath might have a reason in his mind to kill and then to treat a body in a certain way, but once they're done with that corpse, I don't see why they would go to the trouble of digging in what would be tough terrain, in order to dispose of them. Not unless that's going to have an impact on somebody else – like if it's an insult to the deceased, or particularly shocking for those who found it. They're more likely to dump them and be done with it. To me, there's some element of respect being shown here, or the killer thinks the women were witches or demons, and had to be buried in this way without their heads,' Saskia paused a moment, 'but I'm not getting that vibe. There's nothing else at the disposition sites to back that up, although our visit to Dr Chaudhry tomorrow might change my view.'

'Ah yes, breakfast at the morgue. Let's not think about that though.' Winter's eyes seemed to roam her whole face as though he were taking a detailed scan of her, then locked onto her eyes.

She felt her body melting under his gaze.

'So, tell me how you got into all this? What made you want to work in a prison with a bunch of violent criminals and psychopaths?' Winter said it jovially, but to Saskia it was anything but jovial. It was a question she always dreaded because she always had to lie. This time she fudged the truth.

'I knew someone who was nearly killed by a psychopath. When you've seen the consequences of that, it makes you want to do something about it. I also wanted to help offer second chances to those who were dealt a crap hand in life and needed someone to show them a way forward. My work is about finding out why somebody committed an offence and helping them to understand why and to not repeat it so they can go back out into society and live a productive and fulfilling life.'

'Did your parents worry about you going into high security prisons with these people?'

He was fishing – the last time he'd asked about her parents, she'd shut the conversation down fast, just like she always did. 'I don't really keep in touch with my parents. My mum's in Europe somewhere, she's French originally, and I see her occasionally but she moves around. I don't see my dad.'

Winter looked slightly embarrassed. 'I'm sorry. Didn't mean to pry. I'm quite close to my parents – I guess I can't get away from them here on this island.' He laughed, trying to lighten the atmosphere. 'Only child so my mother still loves fussing over me. I don't think she's going to stop until she has grandchildren.' Winter's cheeks flushed as he realised what he'd said.

For Saskia that hammered home again why she could never have a relationship with him. She never wanted children, not when there was a risk that they might inherit the psychopathy that had cursed her brother and father.

Winter's embarrassment was curtailed by the waitress coming back to clear their plates. 'Want to look at the dessert menu?' she asked them both.

'I'm OK, thank you,' Saskia said to her and to Winter.

'Want a coffee or anything?' Winter asked her.

'No. I'm good, thanks.'

'OK, just the bill please,' he said to the waitress and then returned his concentration to Saskia.

There was an awkward silence between them for a few moments.

'I'd better get home and see what that fur ball Bilbo has been up to,' Saskia filled the void. 'I've unlocked his cat flap now we've settled in and he thinks he's Lord of the Manor patrolling the garden and neighbourhood. Never wanders far because he's too lazy, but I don't think the mice in Jersey run very fast because he has been doing quite well at catching them.'

'Do you get them dead or alive?' Winter asked, smiling.

'Various states. Last week's was alive. Took me over an hour to chase it out from behind the sofa and catch it in a Tupperware. Poor thing was petrified but it seemed OK when I let it go.'

'Maybe he'll go and tell his mates to avoid the cat down the road and you'll get fewer deliveries.'

'Let's hope so.' She grinned.

. . .

Driving home in Winter's passenger seat, sitting so close to him, was torture. The wine had pulled down her inhibition wall and her hands itched to reach out to him, to rest on his hard muscular thigh; she could almost feel it under her fingertips. It was almost as though she could feel his body heat, smell his testosterone, and they were pulling her in. This was getting ridiculous. She needed to get a curb on her feelings for him, but not having seen him for a couple of weeks had increased her desire, not lessened it. Like a drug addict missing her fix.

She listened to him talk about work; the latest run-ins with his boss, Detective Chief Inspector Christopher Sharpe, otherwise known as Beak.

'Maybe he's a psychopath,' Winter observed after recounting his story.

'Nah. He's a bit of a narcissist, not a psychopath,' she replied. 'Huge insecurities I'd say. Probably had a lot of put-downs over the years, and has come over here thinking he's the big man.'

'You're not trying to make me feel sorry for him, are you?' Winter stole a glance at her.

'No! Definitely not. Just explaining his attitude.'

A few moments later, Winter pulled up outside her cottage. Dark windows looked back at her and she felt an immediate sadness at having to leave his company and go inside alone. What was this man doing to her? She never worried about being on her own usually; this really was getting out of hand.

'Thanks again for coming to help out at such short notice,' Winter was saying.

Saskia unclipped her seat belt. 'Thanks for dinner.'

'I'll pick you up eight thirty tomorrow. You might perhaps want to skip breakfast until after.'

'You going to offer some of your nice smelling oil to me again?' Saskia's eyes danced over his face, remembering the scented oils he'd offered her when they'd last had to visit a particularly smelly crime scene.

Winter was shadowed, just the headlights of the car leaching into the interior and illuminating the two of them, but she could see the slight stubble of the day on his skin.

His voice changed, taking a softer tone. 'Of course. I've upgraded it since Noirmont. I think I was becoming immune.'

The two of them stared at each other for a few moments before Saskia, realising that they were getting dangerously close to becoming more intimate, broke the atmosphere by fumbling in her rucksack for her house keys.

'I'd better get going she mumbled.' Then dropped the keys in her haste.

Both of them lurched forward to retrieve them from down the side of the passenger seat, their heads colliding.

'Oh my God. Shit, I'm so sorry,' Winter said and reached out to touch her forehead where he'd hit her. 'Have I hurt you?'

Saskia turned to reassure him and found herself inches from his face as he craned to see if the impact had injured her. She could feel his breath on her cheek and the warmth of his hand on her head made her want to melt into it as though she were Bilbo going in for a stroke.

'I'm fine, it was my fault,' she said breathlessly. She had to get out of here before she did something she regretted.

'No, my bad, I should have let you get them.'

She could see the regret in his eyes. He was strong and intelligent, but he was kind. Everything about him was the antithesis of the men who had dominated her life so far. She couldn't help it, the warmth of his personality was magnetic. She wanted him.

'I've got a hard head, I hope you're OK,' she said and put her hand up to his forehead, mirroring his. It was as though a shiver ran through them both and then she couldn't help herself anymore. She kissed him.

She felt his body go rigid with shock initially and then a small groan as he met her lips and their kiss became passionate. It felt as good as she'd anticipated. Like she was being pulled into a whirlpool of warmth that radiated through her body.

What was she thinking?

Saskia pulled away suddenly and grabbed at the handle to get out of the car. 'I'm so sorry. I shouldn't have... I don't know what... I'm sorry,' she said, scrambling to get out of the car.

'No!' Winter tried to reach for her arm, but she pulled it away from his grasp. 'Please, don't. It's OK,' he said. 'I'm fine.'

But it wasn't fine. It was anything but fine. If she'd carried on there would have been no going back. He'd have seeped into every crack of her defences. This man had pulled down the barriers she'd spent years constructing. The walls she'd built up to protect herself. To protect David. To protect anyone she came into contact with. He'd chipped away at them, and in this beautiful island, where the real world could seem a million miles away, she'd allowed herself to relax.

'Saskia, Saskia, please...' she heard Winter call after her and for a few moments, she worried he was going to try to follow her up the cottage path.

He didn't.

As she closed the front door behind her, she saw his face looking at her from the car, confusion and sadness washed across it.

What had she done?

EIGHT

Winter sat in the car, engine still running, staring at Saskia's cottage. He'd just experienced one of the best moments of his life, and one of the worst, all in the space of one minute. What the hell should he do?

His first instinct was to go after her. To knock on her front door and try to speak to her, to tell her he felt exactly the same way. He wanted her as badly as he'd felt she wanted him in that kiss. But something about the stark reality of a closed door in the dead of night held him back. She obviously regretted it. If he went after her, he'd be compounding that regret. The possibility of standing outside knocking on a door that wouldn't open, spoke to his fear of rejection and worries that she might feel as though he were hounding her.

Instead, he texted her. He started writing the message, *I don't regret what you did, I'm glad...* No, that didn't sound right, what if she did regret it, it had all been a mistake and she still only wanted to be friends? He deleted that and started again, *Please don't worry about what just happened, I'm OK.* Shit no, that sounded like she'd just abused him or something, perhaps he shouldn't mention the kiss at all. He started again, *Thank you for your help today and for a lovely evening. I'll pick you up in the morning.* There, that didn't make a big thing of it, would tell her that he wasn't upset about what happened and that she shouldn't be embarrassed. He pressed send.

There was no immediate message back and she didn't appear to be typing anything. The front door remained closed.

Winter sighed and put his car into gear and drove home.

As he drove, his mind and body went back over that kiss a hundred times. The surge that had ripped through him when her lips touched his was like the best wave on the best surf day ever. He had wanted her from almost the first time he'd set eyes on her. Her strength, her intelligence, the way she quietly assessed things and then acted decisively. Her gentleness when it was required, and her calm way of being. The passion he'd just experienced in her, seemed to have come out of nowhere, as though it had burst through some seemingly impenetrable layer of control. He wanted her so badly and for a few moments he felt as though she wanted him too, and yet it was clear there was something holding her back.

By the time he got home, Winter had convinced himself that she had a secret husband back in the UK, or perhaps a serious boyfriend over here. Maybe that's why she'd come to the island. She was so private about her personal life. He had no idea what she did and who she saw when she wasn't at work.

He'd kept glancing over to his mobile phone to see if she'd texted him back but the screen stayed black. Just after he got in, there was a ping and his phone lit up.

It wasn't Saskia. It was Jonno.

> Just seen your message about going to see Chaudhry in the morning, a lift sounds great. See you 8.15.

Damn. He'd forgotten he'd offered Jonno a lift in too. Now what? Should he tell his friend the lift was off? Would Saskia think he'd brought along a chaperone to make sure nothing else happened? Or would she feel relieved that there was someone else in the car to take away the tension? Winter paced up and down his small flat for ten minutes, running through the scenarios in his head. Why was this all so difficult? If he said anything to Jonno then it risked him behaving differently around Saskia and she'd know he'd told him. The woman was too intuitive. He'd have to leave it as it was. Give them both a lift and explain to Saskia that he'd asked Jonno just before they'd gone for dinner. It would be fine. He needed to stop worrying about it and focus on the case.

'So, what's up with you this morning?' Jonno asked five minutes after Winter picked him up.

'Me? Nothing. I'm fine.' Winter could feel his friend's gaze burning into the side of his face as he focused on the road ahead.

'Mate, how long have I known you?'

'Too long.'

'Well cheers, let's just settle at around thirty years shall we? I know that you've got something on your mind. You always go all pinchy-faced and quiet when something's bothering you. Remember that time you broke Miss Morgan's ruler? Nobody knew anything was up except for me. Beak isn't on your back, is he?'

'No, he's not. Everything's fine. I'm not pinchy-faced.' Winter quickly looked at his reflection in the rear-view mirror. 'Just thinking about this case that's all. We don't have much to go on right now and that worries me.'

Jonno didn't reply and Winter could tell from his friend's silence that he hadn't bought his excuse, but wasn't going to push it.

Ten minutes later, they arrived at Saskia's cottage and

Winter could feel the tension in his neck and shoulders. Would she have kept to their plan? Immediately as he pulled up, the door to the cottage opened and she came out. He turned to look up the lane so she didn't think he was staring at her.

Saskia opened the back door and went to get in.

'I can sit in the back and you can come up front if you like?' Jonno said, making as if to get out of the front passenger seat.

'No, you're fine,' Saskia said.

Almost exactly as Winter replied, 'No, you're OK, mate.' He felt Jonno's eyes go from him to Saskia and cursed in his head.

'Morning, Saskia,' he said as cheerfully and as neutrally as he could. 'I texted Jonno before our dinner last night to let him know we were going to Chaudhry's if he wanted a lift.' As he said it, Winter realised that sounded more suspect than not saying anything at all. It came out forced.

'Morning, Winter, Jonno,' she replied.

There was silence for a few moments.

'So, this is where you live,' Jonno said in an overly sing-song cheerful voice. It was more than obvious to Winter that his friend had picked up on the tension. Why hadn't he said he'd just meet him at Chaudhry's? Then he and Saskia could have got the awkwardness out of the way, perhaps talked about what happened. Perhaps agreed that it was something they both wanted. He lived in hope.

'Yes. Just renting, but it's nice,' Saskia was replying from behind him.

'Live on your own?' Jonno asked.

'Apart from my cat, yes.'

Winter felt Jonno's eyes go to his own face again. Blast him. He did know him too well.

. . .

The rest of the journey was thankfully taken up with discussion around the case.

'We've had several reports in from the public about potential IDs for our victims,' Winter told them both. 'One in particular looks promising as more than one person has mentioned this lady's name. A Barbara Smith. Seventy-six-year-old who lives on her own. Hasn't been seen by the neighbours for weeks. Mark and Pete are checking it out this morning.'

'Does she live in the east of the island?' Jonno asked.

'She does. Not too far from one of our disposition sites. No known family in the island either.'

'Why would anyone want to murder an elderly woman like that?' Jonno asked neither of them in particular.

When there was no answer from the back of the car, Winter filled in the silence. 'No idea, but let's hope Dr Chaudhry can give us some clues.'

Dr Chaudhry was as impeccably dressed as he always was, and looked as though he was about to show them around a new house, not two rotting corpses.

'Once you're kitted out, come on straight through, we're ready for you,' he said to all three of them cheerfully.

They pulled on the coveralls and shoe protection that had been left out for them so there was no risk they'd contaminate any evidence attached to the bodies. None of them said a word until Winter took out his little bottle of oil and offered it to Saskia. She hesitated a moment and then held out her wrists.

'Thank you,' she said, but she avoided his eyes.

'What's that?' Jonno asked.

'Scented oils. My secret weapon against pathology lab puking.' Winter tried to make light of it but he could hear the tension in his own voice.

'Bloody hell, you are honoured,' Jonno said to Saskia

jokingly. 'Detective Inspector Winter Labey showing his soft side. Don't mind if I do.' Jonno held out his own wrists to Winter, eyebrows raised and mouth curved into a definite smirk.

Saskia didn't wait for him to finish with Jonno; she walked off in the direction that Dr Chaudhry had taken.

Winter quickly followed, keen to not let Jonno get him alone when he could start quizzing him.

'So, the ladies have an interesting story to tell,' Dr Chaudhry began once they had all assembled. 'I'll start with our first discovery at Mont Ubé, which was actually the most recent burial and therefore in the best condition. The poor woman had at some point been bound. I've found evidence of ligature marks around her wrists and ankles, with bruising and partially healed sores, which suggests that she was held captive for several days prior to death. Traces of food in her stomach contents. I'm thinking soup. It's off for analysis. I'm not going to be able to give you a clear estimate of death because the poor woman was frozen prior to being buried.'

'Frozen?' Jonno asked. 'You mean like put in a freezer or just got cold?'

'I mean like put in a freezer, Detective Sergeant. I can see from her bloods and some burning to her skin and flesh, that she has been in a deep freeze. How long is anybody's guess, but it was long enough for her to freeze right through, so I'm going to say at least two days.'

'Is there any way of knowing if her body was intact at that point?' Winter asked.

'It wasn't. I can see that from the changes to the neck wound. She had also bled out considerably, as you'd expect if decapitated, prior to freezing.'

'And how long had she been buried for?'

'We're still waiting on the full insect data, but I'm going to estimate four to six days.'

Winter was trying hard to focus on the reason they were there, but he couldn't help stealing glances at Saskia. She was concentrating, listening and scanning the victim's body.

'There's no signs of any other injuries to her body, or the application of anything?' she asked Dr Chaudhry.

He turned to her. 'No. Apart from the fact she obviously hadn't been able to bath herself, I've not found traces of any other chemicals or ointments; and no injuries apart from some bruising which was probably as a result of her incarceration and murder. She was held captive, fed and watered, then she was killed, decapitated, frozen, and at some point buried. But... our head tells us more.' He teased them, waggling his eyebrows at them all. A captive audience was his favourite treat.

They followed him over to another metal gurney, where the head of what had once been an older woman, had been placed. Winter felt his stomach tumbling at the sight and averted his eyes. Seeing a lone head like that was even worse than seeing the headless body. He noticed that both Jonno and Saskia were also not too keen on getting close.

'Come on, gather round,' Dr Chaudhry urged them. 'This is important.' He waved them forward, either oblivious or ignoring their discomfort. 'This head belongs to our other body, the first victim killed, but it wasn't buried at the same time. I would say it was interred in-between the first one and the second one. Most importantly, I can see that there is bruising on the lower neck here and on what's left on the body, to see that she was strangled. The other incredibly important fact is that her mouth had been sewn shut.'

'Bloody hell!' Jonno exclaimed and stepped back away from the examination table, bringing the back of his wrist to his mouth and nose.

'Before or after death?' Winter asked, his voice coming out slightly ragged with the effort not to gag.

'Thankfully, a small mercy for this poor woman, after, but literally I would say right after strangulation.'

'Had she been gagged when alive?' Saskia asked.

'Good question, and yes I think there's strong evidence of some kind of gag. The sewing together of the lips has obliterated any signs of it there, but I've seen some discolouration in the skin akin to bruising on the cheeks where something had been drawn tightly around her face. But as you will see–' Dr Chaudhry gesticulated at the head – 'the head wasn't frozen, but it's also not as decayed as the body.' He pointed over to the second corpse behind them, which they'd yet to view. 'This victim's body had also been frozen...'

'What? So the head wasn't frozen but it's also not so decayed?' Winter clarified.

'That's correct, and the reason being is that our killer seems to be somewhat of an amateur taxidermist. He doused the head in formaldehyde. Now as you'll appreciate, there's a lot more to preserving a head than just formaldehyde. He didn't attempt to remove the eyes or brain, any of the soft tissues that would inevitably deteriorate. A half-hearted job to say the least.'

Jonno groaned at this point, forcing back a retch, and stepped even further back from the table.

'Was her head kept in a jar of the fluid you think?' Saskia asked.

'No, I think he treated it, and then kept it out until things started getting a little too smelly, even for him, because despite the chemical, there is insect evidence and also putrefaction. I've also found what looks like damage from some sort of spike that the head has been placed on.'

'But the head was buried after the body?' Winter knitted his eyebrows.

'Yes, from the entomological activity I'd say by a few days, probably a week, maybe two.'

'Eugh, this is so disgusting, so he kept a rotting head for how long?' Jonno asked.

'Indeed, not a man from whom you'd like to accept an invitation for tea at his home. Again we are waiting for all the results to come back and for some X-rays of the fly pupae, but I think the first victim was killed about eight weeks ago. Her body was frozen, the head stayed out and slowly started rotting. The body was probably buried about six weeks ago, the head about three or four.'

'So, quite possibly before the second victim was killed.'

Dr Chaudhry nodded gravely. 'Yes, although we don't obviously know how long she had been frozen for.'

'Have you found anything that connects these two women?'

'Nothing yet. But you should know that both bodies have their legs bent unnaturally backwards, or have signs of them having been bent backwards which fits with them being put into a smaller space than the length of their bodies would normally require in order to be frozen.'

They didn't hang around chatting with the pathologist. Winter guessed that all three of them were on the tipping point of retching and so he made their excuses and left for the fresh air as quickly as he could.

'Sick bastard,' Jonno muttered as they left. 'I mean the killer, not Dr Chaudhry,' he quickly qualified, more to Saskia than Winter.

They all took a moment to breathe in some air.

'I'm not going to get that stench out of my nostrils for days,' Jonno continued.

'I'd better get to work,' Saskia announced, making them both turn and look at her. 'If there's anything else you think would help with my profile, like if you find out who the victims are, could you let me know?'

'Yes, of course. Thank you for coming and sorry to put you through that,' Winter said.

For the first time, she looked at him properly.

'It's fine. I just want to help catch their killer,' she said to him, her face set, and then she turned and left.

Winter watched her back disappearing and wondered if there was some other meaning to what she'd just said.

Jonno bobbed in front of him, interrupting his view with a cheeky smirk on his face.

'So you going to tell me what's going on between you two?'

NINE

TUESDAY

Saskia was mortified with herself, with her own lack of self-control. Why had she kissed him? Well, she knew why, it was because she wanted to, but why had she let herself succumb to the way she felt? Now she'd ruined a perfectly good working relationship and friendship. Part of her had hoped he would come after her, longed for him to continue kissing her the way he'd responded in the car, but when she got the businesslike text from him, she realised he was drawing a line under the incident and didn't want to discuss it further. She'd totally embarrassed herself.

After a tumultuous night's sleep, she woke up determined not to allow it to affect her and the work she was doing with the police. She had a job to do. There were two women who had been murdered; they and their families needed justice. She had to get over herself and just get on with it.

It was harder than she anticipated.

Just seeing him again, and the way he averted his eyes from her, made her want to run away and hide somewhere, just like she used to do when she was afraid of her father; only this time, it wasn't fear of violence that dominated her psyche. He'd even asked his friend along for the journey, clearly didn't trust her to be on her own with him again. What must Winter think of her? Had he told Jonno?

Saskia didn't spend a lot of time worrying about what people thought about her – at least, she hadn't until Winter appeared on the scene – and she was determined to focus on the case and put Winter out of her mind. Her only weak moment came when he got his damned oil out before they went in to the pathology lab. Just being that close to him was almost painful. After that, she shut him out and just focused on the job. Having to deal with the trauma of the two victims, and the visceral reality of their deaths, made that easier.

She felt angry for the way these two women had been treated and murdered. They were alone and would have been terrified, knowing there was unlikely to be anyone who would know they were in trouble and needed help. If there was anything that was going to make her sideline her feelings for Winter, this was it. She wanted justice for these two women, and she wanted to ensure the killer didn't do this to anyone else, because after what she'd just heard, that was her biggest fear.

The more Dr Chaudhry spoke, the more Saskia started to form an outline of the motivation and circumstances of the killer. If they could find out who the victims were, that would be the final piece of information she needed to create her profile. In the meantime, she needed to get away from Winter's presence until the tension between them dissipated. She had her day job to get to, the perfect excuse.

The drive from town to the prison, took around half an hour, most of which was spent with the windscreen wipers at full speed to try to keep the spray and rain at bay as it was propelled by the winds coming straight off the sea.

Heading into work reminded Saskia of the incident with

Richard and Mark Byrne yesterday. She needed to do something about Mark, make sure he knew she was onto him and wasn't going to be threatened. Reporting it officially wasn't an option, not yet. She had no concrete evidence, none of the prisoners would dare speak out against him, and yet if she didn't do something it could end up with someone, quite possibly her, being hurt, maybe even killed. What she needed to do was find out a little bit more about Mark Byrne and his background.

Her opportunity came after one of the team meetings. Mark had been briefly invited to report to the clinical team about one of the prisoners who had been having some issues. Saskia noticed that one of her colleagues, another woman around the same age as her, seemed to find it difficult to engage with Mark. She made sure that she never had eye contact with him, or spoke to him directly. Could she have had a similar experience to Saskia?

When the meeting broke up, Saskia made sure that she left the room with her, walking along the corridor together. She started with small talk.

'Are you finding the new style of the reports easier?' she asked. Since coming to the prison, Saskia had instigated a new system for how concerns were reported. It was a system she'd used in the UK and was simpler and faster than what had been in place with her predecessor.

'I am – it's so much better, takes half the time. Thanks so much for changing that.' Maxine smiled at Saskia as they walked.

'I'm not sure everyone is as happy as you though,' Saskia began. 'I think Mark Byrne prefers the old system.'

There was a pause. 'Yes, but I think any changes aren't going to go down well with him,' she said, dropping her voice slightly.

'What's his background?' Saskia pushed. 'He seems to have been here for ages.'

'He has. Don't think he's ever had another job, this place has been his life. Hasn't even ever moved out of his parents' house.'

'Really?'

'Yeah. Doesn't talk about it much but I heard from someone who went to school with him that his dad was horrible. Died years ago though. I think he was murdered. Maybe that's why Mark works here.'

Saskia's mind was racing. 'Could be. He's not a fan of me, that's for sure,' Saskia said to her, testing.

Maxine stopped and looked at her, as though sizing her up. 'Be careful,' she said dropping her voice even lower to a whisper. 'He has a nasty streak. He's a bully.'

'Yes, I get that impression. Has he ever been hauled up for it?'

Maxine shook her head. 'Most of the staff know to steer clear of him, and none of the prisoners have or will speak up. I've had a few run-ins but he makes sure that there's nothing you can prove; it's always when you're on your own with him and then it's his word against yours.'

'Thanks, I appreciate the warning.'

As soon as Saskia got back to her desk she immediately googled *Byrne death* and discovered that twenty-five years ago, Stuart Byrne was found with head injuries dying in a back alley of St Helier. He was survived by his wife and twenty-year-old son, and nowhere could Saskia find that anyone had been brought to justice for the killing. Was there any possibility that the killer had been Mark? His own son? Perhaps she could get the police to reopen the case. Forensic technology had come on by miles in the past twenty-five years. Saskia stopped herself. She had no new evidence and there was nothing to suggest that Mark could have killed his father, apart from her own intuition and knowledge of his character.

She also realised that her main contact at the police was Winter and right now asking him for a favour wasn't an option.

Perhaps there was another way. Perhaps she just needed to stand up to Mark a bit more and make him realise she wasn't going to be intimidated. Maybe she'd start by going round to his house and making sure he saw her there, just like he'd done to her a few weeks ago. She'd find out his address on the system somehow and go pay him a visit. Start behaving more like a bully herself, than a frightened victim.

It didn't take her long to find his address and, as luck would have it, Mark Byrne and his mother lived not too far from one of the dolmens she'd visited yesterday. The perfect excuse to be strolling around the area, should she need one.

A few hours later, an email arrived in her inbox with Winter's name on it. Her heart and stomach exchanged places in her body.

Hi. Just to let you know we're having a briefing at 5.30 p.m. We've identified one of the victims and so have extra information. Totally understand if you can't make it due to work, but letting you know in the hope you can attend.

In the hope? Was that Winter the police officer or Winter the man who '*hoped*'? Saskia wished it was both but his text last night completely contradicted the kiss that he'd returned. Perhaps he was already seeing someone and had just allowed himself to be seduced by her and then regretted it. Either way, it was good that he'd not tried to take it further. She couldn't and that was that.

Hi Winter, I should be able to make it, will be there for 5.30 p.m. as it will be good to hear the latest.

Best wishes Saskia

She was going for the victims. Winter Labey was a distraction she was going to have to ignore.

The briefing room at Jersey police station was filled. Not surprisingly, the case had created a big stir in the island and with so little to go on, all hands had been drafted in to help with the inquiry. Detective Chief Inspector Chris Sharpe was at the front of the room and when he stood up, a wave of silence travelled along the rows of personnel, reaching Saskia right at the back. She'd told herself she wasn't choosing the very back of the room to be as far away from Winter and Jonno as possible, that it was because she just wanted to listen and wasn't yet ready to contribute, but even she couldn't kid herself.

'Right,' Sharpe began, 'two murder victims, only one complete, buried at three neolithic ritual sites. Do we have a deranged killer on our hands who perhaps has some kind of pagan fetish, or is this a domestic gone wrong? Detective Inspector Labey is lead officer, I'll hand you over to him.' Sharpe nodded at Winter who acknowledged his boss and stood up to face the room.

'As the DCI mentioned, you know the facts. Two bodies, one head, all buried at separate sites. What we also know now is the identify of our first Jane Doe and the site of the first murder. Barbara Smith, seventy-six years of age. Widowed and lived alone, has one son who lives in Australia. We are still trying to track him down before we release her name to the media.' Winter brought up an image of a smiling woman with a kind face on the large digital screen in front of them. A collective sigh rippled through the room at the thought of the violent end she'd had to endure.

'We are trying to find all known associates. We know she went to a book club once a month, and DC Sarah Fuller is tracking down everyone to find out when she was last seen and if any of them could either be suspects, or have any information. She also volunteered for several years with the hospital League of Friends. It was the lady who runs that who contacted us, along with one of Mrs Smith's neighbours, because she hadn't been able to get hold of her and she'd not turned up for a shift. Mark and Pete are just back from Mrs Smith's house where they were able to confirm she was our victim. Anything you can both add?'

Detective Constable Peter Edwards nodded to his senior, Detective Sergeant Mark Le Scelleur, who spoke for them both.

'We attained access to the property through a back door into the kitchen. There were no signs of forced entry. The curtains in the downstairs sitting room window were pulled shut, although the bedroom curtains weren't. This is one of the reasons the neighbour had got concerned. They'd knocked a couple of times and said they were considering calling the police before seeing the appeal for information about our murder victims.'

'Why did they take so long before contacting us if they were concerned? Surely if they thought an elderly woman was in trouble they should have called sooner, she could have been on the floor incapacitated.'

'Yes, that went through their minds, but, and this is the interesting part, they had seen a man in a black uniform, who they assumed was a police officer, visiting the property several times over the previous weeks. His most recent visit was a few weeks ago. They thought perhaps Mrs Smith had been taken ill and was in hospital or a care facility, and the police officer was retrieving items she needed.'

'Presume you are getting them to do a photofit?'

DS Le Scelleur nodded.

'That poses us a problem. If we think there is any possibility that the killer could be a uniformed police officer, then we may need to bring in an outside force to help oversee this investigation.' Winter looked over to DCI Sharpe for guidance.

'Why did they assume he was a police officer? Did he drive a marked car?' the DCI asked.

'No, sir, the neighbours say they never saw a car, and he always came round in the evening when it was dark.'

'Right. So, apart from the fact he could have been disguising himself, he could also be an honorary police officer, or even a security guard, and the fact he's coming round in the evening, suggests to me this man works a day job.'

'Or could just be making sure he's not seen clearly,' Winter added.

DCI Sharpe waved his hand dismissively at Winter. 'Yes, yes, but I'm not escalating this to another police force, handing over our investigation, until we have conclusive evidence which says it might be one of our colleagues. We do, however, have to tread carefully.'

'OK, so we need to get as much information from these neighbours as we can,' Winter said to DS Le Scelleur. 'I assume that door to doors have already been instigated but going forward I want those to be conducted by detectives and not by uniformed police. As from this moment, we need to ensure that all evidence gathering is done by us and no uniformed officers are allowed at any of the crime scenes. Until we can categorically say that the killer cannot be one of our colleagues, then we proceed on the basis that it could be.'

Saskia could see this obviously didn't sit well with the officers in the room who all shuffled and muttered at the prospect. Nobody wanted to think that one of their own could be a killer, but unfortunately, it wasn't unheard of.

'What more can you tell us about what you found at Mrs Smith's house?' Winter asked DS Le Scelleur.

'She had been held captive in her sitting room. There was a chair which had clearly been used for the purpose and evidence of a significant amount of blood on the carpet. We didn't find a freezer that was large enough to accommodate a body.'

'So he's decapitated her there and taken the body and head off site,' Winter thought aloud.

'It didn't look as though there were any signs of decomposition in the room, sir,' Mark Le Scelleur continued. 'Obviously forensics are combing the place now, but to us, it wasn't as if somebody deceased had sat there for some time.'

'So why does he hold his victims captive? Any activity with her bank accounts?' Winter scanned the room.

Detective Constable Sarah Fuller held her arm aloft to get his attention. 'No, sir. I've looked into bank and telephone accounts. All activity ceased two months ago. No phone calls, texts or messages out, and no activity on her bank account.'

'There was also a pile of letters in the hallway, shoved to one side, but that would tally with her not being alive or at liberty, for two months,' DC Pete Edwards added.

'So, Mrs Smith is likely our first victim? And I have to say looking at this image, it tallies with what we saw this morning in the morgue, and also tallies with what Dr Chaudhry has found. All of which intimates that she was taken captive two months ago and killed two weeks later. So how did he choose his victim? Was he known to her? Was there a relationship prior to two months ago or are we looking at an opportunist. The fact she's a woman with no close relatives on the island and clearly leads an independent and quite solitary life, gives me the suspicion that he chose her for that reason. That means he must have known her before. How? Any work been done to the house? Any window cleaners? Postman? This woman must have touched the lives of a multitude of people, what did she do, who did she see, and where did she go apart from the book club and hospital?'

'What about motive? If it's not robbery, what did he want

from her? Have we found any religious or ritualistic evidence?' DCI Sharpe asked Winter and the room.

Winter shook his head. 'Nothing on the body and nothing at the disposition sites, Mark?'

Mark also shook his head. 'Nothing that I could see at her house; it looked perfectly ordinary.'

'So why?' DCI Sharpe pressed. 'Is Saskia Monet going to help us again with a profile?'

Winter's eyes immediately went straight to the back of the room where Saskia stood. She felt them lock onto her and then drop away again immediately.

'Yes, sir. Miss Monet is here at the back. She has kindly agreed to help us again with this investigation.' Winter gave her a small smile and most of the heads in the room swivelled round to look at her.

'Anything you want to add yet, Miss Monet?' DCI Sharpe asked.

She concentrated on him, rather than Winter. 'Not yet, I need to know more about the victim first, but I don't think it's ritualistic. I think the killer was torn between what he did and showing the victim some respect, that's why he buried her at the dolmens. It might not be consecrated ground, but obviously it's hard to get access to a graveyard, and the common belief that only people of importance were buried at these historic sites gives some credence to my theory that he wanted to show her some respect.'

'But why decapitate her?'

'I'm working on that one, but it could be a love-hate relationship with another woman, most likely his own mother, or possibly a partner.'

'Sir, you say we are trying to get hold of the son. Could he have returned from Australia and knocked off his mother?' Detective Constable Fuller asked Winter.

'Good thought, but no I don't believe so. We've checked

with immigration and he is still recorded as being in Australia, but works on a remote ranch so it's just taking us a bit of time to get the news through to him. Also that doesn't fit with there being a second victim. We know she's not a blood relative of Mrs Smith, so why target another woman, and who is she?'

'We might be making some headway with that,' Detective Constable Amanda Potter said. 'There's been a phone call from the library. Sandra Cunningham, seventy-four, and apparently regular as clockwork with her borrowing and bringing back, is late returning some books. Doesn't sound like a big deal I know, but the librarian was insistent that this woman would absolutely not choose to take books back late; plus, they can't get hold of her on the phone. She fits our victim profile and her address is within the area we think the killer is operating.'

'Anyone checked this out yet?'

'I was going to send uniform to visit, but in light of what you said I'll go round there myself. Just get a feeling about this one.'

'I'll come with you,' Winter said to her.

Saskia took that news as her opportunity to slip out quickly before she had to speak to Winter. The more time she could put between *the kissing incident* and when she next had to be in his company, the better. She suspected that he probably felt the same and would be relieved when he saw she'd left.

TEN

Winter and DC Amanda Potter drove towards the parish of St Martin and Sandra Cunningham's house, just as the last of the rain was finally blowing away. Amanda drove, which allowed Winter to sit back and relax for a few minutes, staring out the side window but only half-seeing the granite walls, fields, and houses which appeared and disappeared in a blur. His mind was half on the case and half on Saskia. She'd disappeared really quickly after the briefing. Jonno had already torn a strip off him for the text he'd sent her last night. With the cat out of the bag in terms of something clearly having happened between them, he ended up telling Jonno everything and it had felt good to finally voice the feelings he'd been having for the past few months.

'So that text you sent? Sounded like you just wanted to forget it had ever happened,' Jonno said to him. 'What you on, mate? If you like her and she's clearly expressed that she likes you, then you need to tell her, not pretend like nothing happened. What you scared of?'

'We have a good working relationship. I don't want to lose that if something goes wrong.'

Jonno had sighed deeply at him.

'You're both grown-ups, you can separate out the professional from the personal. You going to spend your life not being with someone you feel strongly about, just because you're afraid of what might happen? Grow a pair, mate, and tell her what you really feel.'

He'd not agreed with his friend immediately, but the words had slowly sunk in and Winter had realised that Jonno was right. Question was, how and when should he do something about it?

Winter parked his own personal problems as the image of the two bodies and severed head from this morning came into his mind. His priority was the two victims right now, and ensuring that nobody else suffered the same fate. He had to focus. They could have been his mother. Two women who were of no threat to anyone, but had been brutally murdered. Why?

Winter cursed himself because as soon as he asked that question, Saskia came into his mind again. He was hoping she'd be able to help him with that question. He pushed her away again. There was one thing he was sure about: she was a complete professional and would no doubt be already formulating a profile for them to use. He needed to get as much information as they could about the victims to her, and it was quite possible that the woman whose house they were currently heading towards, was their second victim.

'Here we are,' Amanda said to him, peering through the windscreen at a small bungalow in an overgrown garden.

Winter looked around the area. 'Those hedges would have hidden the house from any neighbours, and there's nobody right next door to her, so it's a good possibility.'

'She might have just had a turn, or died from natural causes,' Amanda said.

Winter heard the hint of hope in her voice. While they were all wanting to find the identity of their next victim, none of them would wish the fate that had befallen Barbara Smith on someone.

'You're right, and we haven't found the second victim's head yet, but if we are in the right place, this could be pretty gruesome.'

Amanda nodded. Neither of them were looking forward to the next half hour.

Winter led the way up the garden path. It looked as though it had once been cared for but in the last few years had been left to its own devices. Brambles were starting to encroach on the boundaries, and the lawn area clearly hadn't been mown in a long time. The first thing Winter noticed about the house, was that the curtains were closed. That didn't mean foul play; Mrs Cunningham could still have died naturally, or simply have gone away. Or perhaps she liked to close her curtains early. The sky was beginning to darken and the temperature was dropping in readiness for the evening.

He knocked on the front door.

Nothing.

He knocked again. Still nothing.

Winter crouched down and peered through the letter box. It afforded him a view of a hallway with a small table silhouetted against the fading light coming from windows opposite him.

'I'm going to go round the back, looks like the kitchen windows don't have curtains. See if we can see anything.'

Winter and Amanda walked round the side of the bungalow, pushing trailing bushes out of their way.

'This place looks like it has been left abandoned for a while,' Amanda said to him.

'Yes. When did you say the library had seen her last?'

'About six weeks ago.'

'She could have been living somewhere else, or perhaps she

just didn't have the money to get a gardener in. This is a big plot for an elderly woman to manage on her own.'

The kitchen window was an old metal framed window that gave them a good view inside.

'Soup,' was the first thing that Amanda said.

Winter looked and saw several bowls sitting on the kitchen table or in the sink, plus a few opened cans of soup on the side. The hairs on the back of his neck began to rise.

'This doesn't look right,' he said to Amanda. 'Mrs Cunningham? Mrs Cunningham, it's the police. Can you hear me?' he shouted and listened out for any sounds from within.

'Boss,' Amanda said, straining to look inside. 'Is it me, or does that look like a smear of blood on the door there?'

Winter followed her gaze. The kitchen door was painted cream, but there was no mistaking a reddy brown smear on the edge of the door as though someone's fingers had slipped while opening or closing it.

'It could be. Difficult to tell from here. Could just be dried tomato soup,' he said hopefully. His eyes scanned the floor and surfaces for any other signs that things were not as they should be. Right at the end of the hallway, he saw a pile of letters. 'Her post is on the floor, with some of it pushed to one side, just as Mark said they found at Mrs Smith's.' Winter tried the back door. It was locked.

'I'll go see if she has a car in the garage,' Amanda said and immediately walked off to check. Winter tried every window in the hope that one of them might be unlocked. They weren't. He looked up expectantly at the sounds of Amanda's footsteps returning.

'There's a car in the garage,' she said and looked at him, eyebrows raised.

'OK, I think we have reasonable cause to be concerned for Mrs Cunningham's welfare. I think the back door looks like our easiest access point. Let's get some overshoes and gloves on and take a look.'

It didn't take much for Winter to elbow in the glass on the back door and then reach in to turn the lock on the inside. They stepped in, scrunching on the shattered glass.

'Mrs Cunningham? It's the police, can you hear me?' he shouted into the house.

There was nothing except the whirr of the fridge in the silence.

The air smelt stale, but he didn't detect the stench of something else, something like a rotting corpse. Nevertheless, Winter took the lead. If there was a decapitated body in here somewhere, he'd save Amanda the sight of discovering it. Some scenes stayed with you long after the cases were solved and she didn't need that if it wasn't necessary.

Amanda paused to look at the kitchen door. 'I'd say that's blood,' she said behind him.

Winter cautiously walked into the hallway. 'Mrs Cunningham?' To his left, a door was slightly ajar and he could see what looked to be a small sofa underneath the curtained window. He pushed the door with his fingertips, steeling himself. Nothing hit him immediately, but when he turned to look at the armchair opposite the television, he saw the dark brown stains of blood that had soaked into the carpet in front of it, plus some discarded rope and a water cup.

'Get onto forensics,' he said to Amanda. 'This tallies with what they found at Mrs Smith's house.'

Amanda stood in the hallway talking on her mobile phone while Winter crossed to one of the doors on the right-hand side.

Careful to touch the handle as little as possible so as not to disturb prints, he opened the door. It was the bedroom. A pink flowery throw was on the bed, which was made up with sheets and blankets. The room was tidy enough; it looked as though Mrs Cunningham had got up, dressed and then just disappeared. In fact, what she must have done is got up and unsuspectingly opened the door to her attacker. With no signs of forced entry, she either knew him, or he'd overpowered her once the door was open. Then, he'd tied her to her chair before killing her.

Winter crossed to the dressing table and looked in the jewellery box on top. It didn't look as though it had been touched. Where was her handbag? Perhaps she'd made a note of an appointment. He did a quick scan of the bedroom, not seeing anything else of interest, and exited back into the hallway. Amanda was just finishing up on the phone call to the office. Winter opened the third and final door. It turned out to be the bathroom and toilet. Again, there was nothing obviously untoward.

'I want to find her handbag, see if she made any notes about an appointment. Can you check in the kitchen to see if there's a calendar or anything like that?'

'Sure.' Amanda headed straight off.

Winter walked to where Mrs Cunningham had been held captive in her own armchair. A place where she would have felt safe, but which was ultimately the scene of her own brutal murder. An incongruously comfortable-looking reclining chair, which was now soiled and stained. No doubt the poor woman would have sat waiting to be allowed to go to the toilet. He imagined her fear and shame as she sat waiting for her attacker. Did he come and go, leaving her here alone, bound and gagged, or did he live in the house with her, torturing her with his presence as he built up to the final act?

To one side of the chair was a magazine rack with the TV remote perched on top. He skirted around the blood in front; a red handbag rested on the floor on the other side. Winter picked it up and carried it over to the sofa. Inside was a small mobile phone, one that simply made calls and texts. He tried to turn it on, but it stayed dead. The battery had no doubt run out. There was a variety of items he'd expect to find in an elderly woman's handbag: lipstick, tissues, a foldaway shopping bag, a small address book, and a notebook and pen. He looked through the notebook, hoping that he'd find a clue. A message by Mrs Cunningham from beyond the grave, helping lead them to her killer. It was mostly shopping lists and what appeared to be the titles of books.

'Found a calendar,' Amanda said as she came back into the living room brandishing a slimline wall calendar with images of various birds. 'There's a few entries for the last couple of months, one that says *M to fix porch light*, which might be a potential lead.'

'OK. Good. Bag it up and we'll see if we can cross-reference it with her address book and phone. Until we get conclusive DNA evidence to say that Mrs Cunningham is our corpse in the morgue, we have to keep an open mind, but the evidence certainly says she is to me.'

'Yes.' Amanda slowly nodded, staring sadly at the armchair. 'I can't see any other explanation for the blood and mess.'

Winter's eyes were caught by a photograph on the bookshelf. A smiling elderly woman sitting on a bench in Howard Davis Park, with an elderly man. Was that Mrs Cunningham and her husband in happier times? A moment long before the events of the last few weeks, when she would never have been able to contemplate what was to happen and how she would meet her death.

Winter snapped back into business mode.

'Can you get started on door to doors? People should be getting home from work now. Get Pete to come out and help you, and remember we need to keep uniform out of here until we can put that possibility to rest. I'll hang on here until forensics come and see if I can find anything else.'

'You seriously think one of our own could have done this?'

'Mandy, you and I both know that some successful criminals have been police officers. They know how to avoid capture and they're trusted. I can't say for sure that it's not, but I certainly am hoping it isn't. Either way, we have to play this by the book so that we don't compromise a conviction, or get accused of harbouring the individual.'

'I don't think any of us would harbour them, I'd like to string him up for what he's done to these women,' she replied, the last few words dropping almost to a mutter.

Winter heard what she said and despite agreeing with her, chose to just ignore the sentiment for now. If it did turn out that one of their officers was responsible, he'd have to cross that bridge when he came to it. Right now he just wanted to stop this man and make sure that Mrs Cunningham was the last of his victims.

ELEVEN

Saskia drove home and arrived in St Ouen's Bay just in time to see the sky come alive with orange as the sun headed to bed. On a whim, she turned her car into one of the car parks and pulled up facing the beach, looking at the dark grey sea and its alter ego above. Soon, they would merge into one in the distance as the sky returned to darkness, speckled only with a few stars and a sliver of moon that would dance in the waves below. She needed this. Nature. The wholesome goodness of it, the grounding knowledge that whatever the day had been like, there was something far greater and more powerful than her and all those she'd had to deal with. The brutal killer of two elderly women, Mark Byrne, her own shame at her behaviour towards Winter, and her brother. All of that became insignificant in the face of this view.

She didn't get out of the car; instead she allowed her shoulders to drop and relax, and just breathed. Saskia had started to feel happy and comfortable in the last few months. She'd spent her entire life on edge. At first terrified of her father, living on a knife point every day, never knowing what violence might enter her world. Once he'd been taken away, she had the emotional fallout of her mother and the growing behavioural problems of her brother to deal with. They'd been forced to move regularly, sometimes because they couldn't afford the rent, other times because neighbours had found out who they were – the family of the Nightingale Strangler, and they were targeted.

Once, Saskia had been chased and corralled in a disused warehouse by several older boys from down her street. They'd discussed whether to cut her, or beat her, and then one of them had suggested they rape her. She'd seen the animal look on their faces, their inhuman eyes when they stared at her, and she'd gone into the same defensive mode she'd had to use against her father. There was no way she could fight them; she was tough, but not against four older boys, so she'd used her brain to get herself out of the situation. Instead of pleading for mercy, she'd gone into a crazy state, and then fallen on the floor as though she was having a fit. It had worked. The boys, fearful that she was dying, had run away. She hadn't told her mother, but she did warn her brother. The following week one of the boys had been found with a metal skewer embedded in his stomach. He'd survived, but he'd been too scared to tell the police that it had been David who'd done it, and too ashamed to tell others that a kid four years younger than him had got the better of him. None of them touched her or taunted her again after that.

In those days, it was a fight for survival and Saskia had overlooked David's aggression. It was them against the world. Things were different now. David was a grown man who had learnt to manipulate and lie in order to get what he wanted, and his complete disregard for others now had far greater consequence. Saskia understood what was right and what was wrong. She heard about the consequences and the victims of violence every day in her job. That early survival instinct had given way to a crusading one. She wanted to prevent there being more victims. That's why the situation with David now was causing her stress.

Saskia felt her neck and shoulders tense. David was due round that evening for their weekly session. Her fears over what had occurred with Allan wouldn't go away. The police might have charged Kevin for the murder, but the diamond necklace had planted doubts in her mind that just wouldn't be quietened. She was going to have to confront him again this evening, and try to find out, one way or another, if he could have been responsible. Saskia didn't want to have to think about what she'd need to do if he was, but she knew there were others who might be in danger if she didn't act.

Bilbo's face at the dark window of her sitting room, made her smile. She wondered if he'd bothered to get up at all from his comfy cushion, since she'd left him that morning. Once she'd got in through the front door and seen the coating of cat hairs on her chair, she got her answer.

Bilbo meowed and weaved his way around her ankles, reminding her that his dinner should be her first priority. Saskia hadn't missed the glance that Jonno had given Winter that morning when they'd picked her up. He'd asked if she lived alone and she'd mentioned Bilbo. What had they discussed before she got in that car? Whatever it was, she'd shake it off. She'd had to deal with far worse.

David was due in half an hour, so she fed Bilbo, got changed, and started preparing her dinner so it could be cooking while he was here.

Half an hour after he'd been due, her dinner was bubbling away in the oven and so she'd texted him. Being late was no surprise – he didn't care about making people wait – but she needed to know if he was going to be another half hour, or longer, as that would determine when she ate.

As soon as she'd sent the text, she saw that he was typing back.

> Can't make it tonight. See you next week.

Saskia frowned and replied.

> Can't you do tomorrow or Thursday?

> No busy.

It wasn't impossible that David was busy, he and Jackie had quite an active social life, but Saskia needed to put her mind to rest about the Allan situation. The longer she left it, the longer it festered in the back of her head.

> Weekend?

There was no reply. Not immediately, not an hour later, not even by the time she went to bed. Instead, she'd sat eating her dinner alone, thinking about David, Winter, Mark Byrne, and who the killer of two innocent women could be.

TWELVE

He'd often wondered what his life might be like if there wasn't a television in their house. She had it on permanently, hopping between channels to watch all her favourites. They didn't have anything fancy, not like people talked about at work: that Sky and Netflix or, heaven-forbid, Disney Channel, but there was enough to keep her happy. That box saved his life because it kept her focus away from him. Every week he had to buy her the *Radio Times* and she would sit there, highlighting her programmes, looking for gaps in her viewing.

It was leek and potato soup tonight, followed by a Co-op ready meal of liver and bacon with mash. Potato overload, but she rarely even looked at her food, let alone commented on it. She sat there staring at the TV screen, shovelling whatever was on the plate into her mouth. It was the way he liked it because that meant her mouth was silenced. Although never for long.

'Where's my milk?' she'd snarked at him, without even looking his way.

'I have it ready, I'll bring it now,' he'd replied, quickly heading into the kitchen where the glass was on the side.

'Always forgetting something. Brain dead, that's you, just like your father. No wonder you never amounted to much.'

He handed her the glass and bit his tongue. He knew better, even if he also knew that he'd not forgotten the milk.

Afterwards, he'd emptied the commode in her bedroom, ready for bedtime. She always had to get up to use the toilet overnight and she didn't want to have to walk to the bathroom, so she'd made him get a commode to put by the bed. It made him gag sometimes as he emptied it. He flushed it out with some floral smelling antibacterial liquid and then replaced it, ready for the night ahead.

Then, one final glance into the sitting room where the light flickered onto her sallow sagging skin from the TV, and he was free. Free to go and visit his friends.

They always started off grateful. Lots of thank yous and smiles. Sometimes a cake baked or a tenner pressed into his hand. He'd helped her to secure one of her windows after some hooligan had put his fist through it. He knew she didn't have much money, and she didn't want to have to be bothered with the hassle of claiming on insurance, so he'd sorted it for her. This evening, he'd promised to replace the bulb in her outside light for her. He didn't want her tripping over and ending up in hospital.

After he knocked and saw the outline of her come towards the front door through the frosted glass, he called out to reassure her.

'It's alright, Mrs Baxter, it's me.'

She unlocked the door, smiling, and waved him in. She enjoyed his company, wanted to be around him. When she looked at him there was no disgust or hatred, just gratitude. This was what he needed. Motherly gratitude.

'Would you like a cup of tea?' she asked him.

'That would be nice, thank you.'

'Milk and one sugar?'

He smiled. She remembered. 'Yes.'

He'd bought the bulb earlier that day and he had it with him.

'Let me know how much I owe you for that,' she said as he pulled it out of his pocket.

'Don't you worry about that.' He didn't mind spending a few pounds to help her. She liked him. She was his friend. To stop her trying to persuade him, he went out the back door and set to work unscrewing the light fitting to replace the bulb, whistling while he did it.

He liked watching her through the window. She couldn't see much out to the dark garden, but he could see her. She was busying around the kitchen, making the tea and putting some little cakes on a plate. Mrs Cunningham had been like that, soft and gentle and grateful for his help. But she ruined it. They usually did eventually.

After he'd sorted the bulb, he would go inside and they would sit and chat for a bit. Mrs Baxter talked to him like she was actually interested in what he said and was doing. She'd offer more tea. He'd decline and say he had to get back, he had something to do.

He enjoyed his visits.

She was a good mother to him.

The kind of mother he deserved.

If only things would stay that way.

THIRTEEN

David didn't bother replying to Saskia's question about the weekend. He didn't want to go and see her this week and that was that. In fact, he didn't think he needed their sessions at all anymore. He had it sorted. He was beginning to get annoyed with her intrusive questions. It was his life and he was entitled to live it how he wanted. It had nothing to do with her.

Things were progressing well with Jackie. They'd been due to go out with her friends, Roger and Diane, tonight, but David had made sure he was at home when she came in. He'd told Steven Wood, his so-called boss, that he was working from home. They were entitled to flexi-working – it was in the contract. He'd chilled a bottle of champagne and when Jackie's taxi pulled into the courtyard, he'd poured her a glass, adding one of the sleeping pills he'd bought off the internet.

She'd been so appreciative when he'd greeted her with bubbles and a kiss. Even more so when he'd suggested a quick massage to ease her stress from the day, before they went out.

'You've been so tired lately, a lot on your mind,' he'd said to her.

'Have I?'

He'd half smiled sympathetically at her.

'You mean forgetful,' she'd replied sighing. 'Yeah I don't know what's the matter with me. It's ever since Allan was murdered. I'm struggling to concentrate.'

'Maybe we should take ourselves off on a nice holiday,' he'd said, rubbing her shoulders as he watched her sip at the champagne.

'Yeah, maybe you're right, that's what I need. The situation with Mum is hardly helping.'

'Head upstairs and take your work clothes off and I'll come and give you a quick massage. We're not due out until eight. You finish your champagne and I'll get you another glass.'

Jackie had necked the rest of the champagne and while she'd gone upstairs, he'd returned to the kitchen, filling up her glass. One pill should be enough for what he needed. He didn't want to totally knock her out. He looked out the kitchen window to the dark, empty flat above the garage where Allan had lived. Killing him had been pleasurable, and the satisfaction had been increased by knowing he'd been so clever in framing Kevin, Allan's boyfriend, for the murder. Just the thought of it excited him.

His mind went to Jackie upstairs. She was putty in his hands. They wouldn't be seeing Roger and Diane tonight. They were as boring as hell and he couldn't be bothered. Jackie would call and make her excuses because she was simply too tired, and they'd know that she wasn't her usual self. When eventually Jackie takes her own life, it would come as no surprise to any of her friends. He'd make sure of that.

The thought of it all aroused him.

By the time he went upstairs, she was already lying on the bed. He increased the heat in the bedroom and warmed up the oil in his hands, before gently massaging her shoulders. Half an hour later, she was unable to keep her eyes open.

'We'd better get dressed and out,' David said to her, heading into the bathroom to wash the oil from his hands.

Behind him, he heard Jackie groan.

'Darling, if you don't feel up to it, we can call them and make our excuses. I can just cook you a little something and you can get an early night.'

'I don't know, it's letting them down.'

'They're your friends, sweetheart, they will understand.'

'Yeah, course. You're right. I just can't face getting dressed and going back out again. Can you pass me my phone?'

'Sure, here you go.'

David went back into the bathroom so it wouldn't look as though he was hanging around listening to her phone call.

'Diane, it's Jackie. Look I'm so sorry to do this to you, but I'm just not up to going out tonight... No I'll be fine, just tired that's all. I hope you both have a lovely evening... Yeah, speak soon.' Jackie groaned again as she put the phone down. 'I could sleep for a week.'

'Would you like me to bring you something up, or do you want to come downstairs?' David asked, appearing from the bathroom. He sat on the edge of the bed and took her hand, caressing the back of it. 'Perhaps you're coming down with something.'

'Maybe. You know, I don't feel that hungry. I think I'll just go straight to sleep. I really don't feel like I can keep my eyes open any longer.'

'OK, sweetheart, but you know where I am if you need anything.'

He left her to it. News would travel around her friends that she'd bailed on them, and when she did it again, another night, as she would, they'd really start to notice. If he had his way, he'd be hastening the process with some other drugs or poison, but at her age there would be bound to be an autopsy. He needed this to look good, for her to marry him and put him in her will, if he was to get what he wanted. It would take longer, but he could wait.

FOURTEEN

It was late by the time Winter was able to leave Sandra Cunningham's house. There was no sign of the victim's head at the scene, and he'd asked two of his detectives to go back and check every one of the dolmens again, just in case the killer had returned and buried it after they'd finished the initial examination. There was no sign of it.

His biggest hope was to find fingerprints and DNA evidence at the murder scene. None of the neighbours had noticed anything or anyone.

'We never really saw her much,' one woman had said, her mind clearly not on the subject of the conversation and instead drifting back to the television where some reality TV show was on. Winter felt a sadness for Sandra Cunningham, a woman he'd never met but who had clearly lived a lonely existence. She'd never had children and her husband had been dead for eight years. No wonder her library visits had been so important to her. She may have received very little care and attention in her life, but he was damned sure he was going to bring whoever had killed her to justice.

He went home via the local Co-op at Five Oaks, picking up

something quick and easy. He knew ready meals weren't good for him – ultra-processed crap his mother called them, and she was right, but needs must. He was just too damned tired to cook from scratch.

Winter checked in with the office while the microwave got his dinner ready for him. The door to doors hadn't brought up anything new and there were no new leads either. It amazed him how on such a small island someone could kill, people could disappear, and nobody see a thing.

While he ate, his mind went back to his favourite distraction, Saskia. He was thinking about calling her, but by the time he'd finished his decidedly average ready meal, it was gone ten p.m. and it felt too late. Instead, he emailed her to let her know they'd almost certainly found the identity of the second victim. They'd know by morning hopefully, from fingerprints, but it would be a few days before the full DNA results came through.

It was ridiculous, but it took him ages to write the email. He chose every word carefully, worried that she'd read something else between the lines. He was going to have to talk to her about this, have an adult conversation instead of behaving like a lovesick teenager. He just hoped she didn't regret what she'd done.

After he fell asleep on the sofa in front of the ten o'clock news, Winter dragged himself to bed, exhausted. His alarm was set for seven a.m. and his tired brain needed a good sleep to process the huge amount of information and clues that he'd taken on board today. He fell asleep quickly but woke himself up shouting in a nightmare. His mother was being buried alive at a dolmen site by a crazed man dressed in black, and Saskia was standing watching and crying. He couldn't reach either of them and he knew that Saskia would be next. Winter did what he always did when work nightmares woke him: he closed his eyes and imagined he was at St Ouen on the surf, riding the perfect wave with the sound of the sea and the smell of the salt all around him.

Winter's sleep tactic clearly worked because the next thing he was aware of was the alarm going off. That's not to say that he didn't have more nightmares, he knew he had because his body didn't feel rested and there was a sadness to the morning. He jumped in the shower, made himself a couple of eggs on a bagel for breakfast, and then headed into the office, turning the music up loud in the car to try to shake off the blues.

He would have missed his phone ringing, if it hadn't interrupted the music.

'Boss,' it was Detective Constable Everton on the phone, 'a head's been found at Hougue Bie.'

Winter turned his car and drove to the ancient site, his mood now completely irreversible. He prayed that it might at least be the remains of Sandra Cunningham and that they didn't have another victim to add to the tally.

La Hougue Bie is one of the ten oldest human structures in the world. A Neolithic passage grave and ritual site, which aligns with the rising sun at the spring and summer equinoxes, and was built around 4,000–3,500 BC. Six thousand years later, the site was excavated and now the passageway is open for visitors to crawl into. A small sixteenth-century chapel – Christianity's attempt to supersede the pagan site – remains on top of the mound like a barnacle piggybacking a turtle shell. Winter wondered if the head was inside the mound or in the chapel. This time the killer had an option, pagan or Christian, and perhaps his choice might give them a clue.

The mound was clear to see as he drove along Princes Tower Road towards the Jersey Heritage site. As he pulled into the car park, the police presence was just as obvious. A forensic team van had disgorged its occupants and there were two Jersey

Heritage staff standing talking to Jonno. There was much shaking of heads.

Jonno spotted Winter arriving and walked over as he got out of his car.

'Morning. This is the killer who keeps on giving,' his friend said to him with his usual dry humour.

'Any indications as to who the remains belong to?'

'From the photograph I've seen, it's highly possible that it's Sandra Cunningham, but obviously I've not seen it myself.'

Winter could tell from Jonno's tone of voice that he was hoping he didn't have to see it either.

'So what happened? How was it found? And how did he get in here? Surely this place gets locked up at night?'

'It does, and there was an alarm tripped at about one a.m. There's on-site security and he was backed up by the honorary police and a couple of our lads attended. They searched the entire site and found nothing and nobody.'

'Where was the head found?'

'In the burial chamber under the mound. I've been assured by Scott Askew, who was one of the uniforms attending, that he looked and saw nothing. Scott's a good bloke,' Jonno added in response to the look from Winter. They both knew that there was a question mark over whether someone in uniform was involved.

'So you're thinking that whoever it was hid and then deposited her after they'd left?'

Jonno shrugged. 'I'm not sure, but if that is the case, why didn't the alarms go off again or why weren't they captured on CCTV?'

'What are you saying?'

'I'm saying that the cameras caught nobody running around with a human head either before or after the alarms went off.'

'There must be a blind spot.'

'That's what I was just discussing with Lewis, the site

guardian. He reckons there isn't. You're talking about an extremely important historical structure, they've got it covered.'

Winter frowned. 'I want the names of everyone who attended last night, and all staff, plus all the camera footage.'

'On it,' Jonno said to his back as Winter strode off towards the mound.

The entrance to the chamber was on the opposite side to the car park. On his right was the mound, to the left the museum building. Winter was still frowning as he reached the entrance to the burial chamber. Small, granite stones were built into the lower part of the exposed bank. It resembled a large green cake or round cheese that had a slice taken from it so that you could see inside the grassy outer layer. In the centre, at the point of the removed slice, was a small square hole that was large enough for an adult to crouch down and enter. Winter knew from the many visits here as a child, and since, that the chamber got larger towards the end, enabling a man to stand up. Usually the entrance was dark but today bright light shone out of it instead of into it, evidence of the forensic investigation lamps that had been taken inside.

He stood for a moment contemplating why the killer kept choosing the neolithic burial chambers in which to dispose of the bodies and heads. The back of the little chapel on top of the mound was up above Winter. If the only reason why the dolmens had been chosen was because of the lack of access to Christian sites, then surely the killer would have walked up the mound and left the head there? Or perhaps that left him more exposed.

Winter became aware of a noise coming from the burial chamber that wasn't far from the sound of a grunting warthog; somebody was clearly struggling with the limbo-esque method of entry and exit.

Dr Imran Chaudhry's head appeared seconds later.

'Dr Chaudhry,' Winter said, unable to control the small

smile that had crept onto his lips at the sight of the pathologist exiting into daylight like a creature from the *Wind in the Willows*, or a Roald Dahl book.

'Why couldn't they build the bloody things full height,' Dr Chaudhry said as he straightened up in the daylight. 'Good job I'm not claustrophobic.'

'Sorry to put you through that,' Winter said, still trying to suppress the smile.

Dr Chaudhry humphed. 'Looks like the missing head for our body in the morgue. Same as for the other poor woman. Mouth sewn up and it's been treated haphazardly with formaldehyde.'

'Any attempt to bury it?'

'No, looks like it's literally been thrown in there like a bowling ball from the dust and gravel impact on her.'

'So done in a rush you'd say?'

'I'd say yes, but you're the detective, aren't you going to take a look?'

'I will be, just getting the lay of the land out here first,' Winter said.

Dr Chaudhry gave him a look which clearly said that he knew Winter wasn't keen on going in there and was making up excuses.

'I'll get preliminaries to you later today, but I'd be surprised if it's not a fit to our headless body.'

'Thank you, Dr Chaudhry, I do appreciate you coming out here like this.'

Chaudhry humphed again and walked off with a wave of his hand.

Winter hung around the entrance for a little longer just taking in the site. It never ceased to amaze him how accurate these ancient people had been when they built the passage and chamber, one of the longest in Western Europe. They'd known the exact path that the sun would take at the equinox and had the organisational knowledge and strength to drag the huge stones needed to build it up from the coastline where they originated. Six thousand years ago they would have celebrated their dead, carried out rituals and ceremonies here. Just like the other dolmen sites, why would the killer want to bring his victims here?

Winter turned and looked at the site boundary and contemplated its position with roads on three sides. Then he looked back at the entrance into the chamber and sighed. He was going to have to go in and see for himself.

To get inside, he had to bend double, shuffling into the passageway. He could see someone kneeling down around three quarters of the way along, before the main chamber. Big upright granite stones lined the walls, with huge flat granite stones lying across them to create the ceiling. It was sobering to know that there were tons and tons of stones, earth and chapel, above his head, all held up by a neolithic structure that had been doing so for thousands of years.

'DI Labey, fancy seeing you here,' the crouching figure said to him.

Winter couldn't see the man's face as the light from behind had turned him into a silhouette, but he recognised the voice.

'Andrew, what have we got?' Winter was relieved to find that he'd reached a spot where the ceiling was higher and he could stand up.

'The head of a woman, which looks as though somebody has tossed it in here. She had come to rest partially obscured from the entrance by one of the standing stones here. I know there's been some talk about why she wasn't spotted last night when the alarm went off, but as you'll see from the photographs we've taken, she wasn't fully visible and quite frankly, who would have been looking for just a head anyway? It would have looked like a stone from outside.'

'How was she found then?'

'An unfortunate French tourist who is now receiving treatment in the hospital. He'd arrived first thing this morning, crawled in here and came face to face with her, literally. The site guardian heard his screams and had to drag the poor fellow out by his feet as he'd jumped up and whacked his head on the ceiling, knocking himself out. Dare say he won't be visiting anymore Pagan burial chambers. Probably going to need therapy.'

Winter heard the slight humour in Andrew's voice. If Jonno's sense of humour was dry, then Andrew Picot's was positively dehydrated.

'Anything else you can tell me?'

'Not much. I don't think your man came in here at all; we'd be hard pressed to find anything like fingerprints and footprints in the gravel and on the stones anyway.' Andrew paused. 'The poor woman was tossed in here, probably by her hair, like a bowling ball.' Winter heard the humanity in Andrew's voice.

'Thanks,' Winter replied, beginning to feel a little claustrophobic at the thought of a head flying in and then rolling at his feet. The head itself didn't look real. It was like a bad Halloween prop where the rubber had started to rot. He tried not to look at it too much, but from the photographs they'd found in Sandra Cunningham's house yesterday, he would wager that this was the final part of her mortal remains. He felt anger at not only the needless manner of her death, but also the lack of respect she'd been shown.

'Have you checked further up?' He nodded towards the back of the passageway.

'Yup, nothing that we can see,' Andrew said to him.

Winter sidled past Andrew in the cramped passageway, until he reached the main chamber where he could stand up. At the very back was a raised area and then the terminal cell. This was the most sacred part of the whole formation, standing stones formed a small area that was divided from the rest of it, like a small changing cubicle, and had once perhaps been where the shaman or spiritual leader would prepare themself for the ceremonies. It was large enough for somebody to hide in and not be seen if a torch was shone down the passageway. There were also two side chambers just prior to the raised area, places where the dead would be put.

Winter bent double again and shuffled along the gravel floor past Andrew and towards the exit. The prospect of getting outside into the fresh air and open spaces, spurred him along. At other times when he'd come into the passageway and chamber, he felt the sense of awe and mysticism of the neolithic ritual site. Today, with the forensic lights bleaching the granite stones white, chasing away the ancient shadows and aura of pagan ceremony, it was another crime scene and one he would quite like to leave behind.

He stood up straight and breathed in the fresh air as soon as he was clear of the chamber, then Winter strolled around the rest of the site looking for hiding places and potential entrances and exits. He walked up the winding path of the mound, towards the chapel, built in the twelfth century and modified a few centuries later by the Dean of Jersey who performed fake miracles to persuade pilgrims to part with their cash. At its base was the little crypt the Dean had built, where someone could have hidden, as well as the two rooms of the main chapel.

From the top, Winter could look down on the whole site. It was a small area, but there was not just plenty of history, but also hiding places. The museum buildings would have definitely been locked and alarmed, so too would the underground tunnels built by the Germans during the occupation of the island in World War II. These were now a monument to the slave workers who had died and suffered in building the enemy fortifications across Jersey and the other Channel Islands. In the grounds there was also a medieval long house – a replica built by volunteers – as well as another building which housed the tearoom and toilets.

But with five men searching the site, they still should have been able to find anyone hiding – and most of the buildings would have been locked and inaccessible. The security cameras would have picked up someone running around avoiding detection.

From what Andrew had said, it was quite possible that the head was already in the dolmen when the officers checked the chamber. They would have been looking for an entire person, not just a head, so it would have been easy to miss. Andrew was right, their killer hadn't made the journey inside. If he had, he'd have put the head in one of the side chambers or on the raised platform at the end. This was a hurried disposal, unlike the others where he'd dug in difficult ground. There was also no way the head could have been thrown in from the roadside, so the killer had accessed the site somehow. Had he been surprised when he set off the alarms? The first site where the killer had come up against cameras and security. Winter picked up his pace and headed back to Jonno. They had work to do.

FIFTEEN
WEDNESDAY

When Saskia received the email from Winter, she'd cussed at herself for the way she'd pounced on it like a schoolgirl with a crush. He was as professional as ever, passing on information which could help her with her profile of the killer. They'd identified the second victim and the second head had been found at Hougue Bie overnight.

Saskia was building up a picture of who the killer was and his motivations, although she wasn't yet quite ready to share her thoughts. Later she was going to sit down and pull everything together into a profile and a report, then she could step back from the investigation and she wouldn't need to be in Winter's presence again.

She had a run of meetings at work in the morning, one or two that she'd put off due to helping out yesterday, and so she couldn't postpone them again. She told herself to focus on work and forget about DI Winter Labey. It was not a relationship that was going to go anywhere other than on a professional level and even that might have been compromised.

Her first meeting went fine. It was a Teams meeting with colleagues from other support and welfare organisations, talking about a couple of the prisoners who were due for release shortly. It dragged on slightly longer than she'd hoped and she found herself rushing to get to the next meeting, which was in person at the prison.

Saskia entered the meeting room around ten minutes late and everyone turned to look at her. Most of the faces were friendly and wished her good morning as she made her apologies, but one was not. Mark Byrne was there, his big bulk sitting across the table, arms folded and a look of disdain on his bearded face. The only available chair was right in front of him. Saskia gave herself a mental boot up the backside and tried to show no element of the way she felt about sitting looking at that man. Luckily for her, she'd learnt from two of the best when it came to deceit and hiding your true feelings, so she'd sat down, smiling at him, and turned her focus onto her colleague who was talking.

Mark kept staring at her. She could feel his eyes watching her like hot pokers trying to prod her into looking back at him. Fifteen minutes into the meeting, he shifted in his seat and kicked his leg out, right into her shin. It hurt. He was wearing hard boots and her shin was not padded.

The prison governor was in full flow about a new project that was being proposed, so Saskia didn't want to make a fuss. Instead she looked over at Mark Byrne to glare at him, but he'd turned away, a slight smirk on his face.

Saskia was taken back to her school days when the bullies had picked on her then. Only she wasn't a child anymore and she wasn't going to take Byrne's aggression lying down. She kept her legs well out of his reach for the rest of the meeting, the spot on her shin where he'd kicked her throbbing throughout. She was under no illusion that it had been deliberate and not an accidental knock.

Saskia was surprised by how emotional the incident made her. There was so much negativity going on in her life that this was one more slap down. The situation with David, the awkwardness with Winter, there seemed no let up to it. She felt herself becoming a social pariah again, recognising that she was withdrawing further from people, just like she had as a child.

When she got back to her office, she lifted up her trouser leg to view her shin. It was already a deep shade of red and would no doubt be purple within the next day or so. She'd survive, and it wasn't the bruise that was upsetting her, it was the unnecessary bullying. But, she hadn't worked in the prison service for this long without dealing with men like Mark Byrne. Experience had taught her that lashing out would be ineffectual. She had to bide her time and her chance would come.

Saskia texted David again to ask when he would be coming round. He didn't reply. Alarm bells were ringing in her head about her brother. If he felt like he could manage without her, without their sessions, then that could mean he was starting to lose his grip on what society expected of him. Without constant reinforcement, he could revert to psychopathic type and that would ultimately be dangerous for somebody.

Her thoughts turned to their mother. She hadn't heard from her in a while. Their last conversation had been rushed, her mum heading off for a train to somewhere in the Alps where she was going to work at a ski resort. Perhaps she'd finally met a nice man, but Saskia doubted it. Her mother was too badly scarred by her father for her to ever be able to trust anyone again. David hated her. Called her weak and pathetic. He was his father's son for sure.

Saskia had only just managed to save her mother's life by calling the police and stopping her dad from strangling their mother, but it was as though he'd transferred that onto David. David had watched the whole incident when he was just a few years old. Now his mother was terrified of him and had made Saskia swear she would never tell him where she was. It's why she kept moving, never staying anywhere longer than a few months. Always looking over her shoulder.

Winter came back into Saskia's mind. Not that he was ever long out of it. He seemed so grounded and secure in his life. No doubt his parents were a huge factor in that. She'd seen the results of poor parenting and no parenting, so often in the prisons. How people start off is a critical factor in antisocial behaviour. Without clear role models and boundaries, young people were more likely to grow up to be adults who didn't understand society's expectations and were unable to reach their potential. It was tragic seeing some of the young men in the jails, men who had they been given some love and guidance in their early years, would have become happy adults with jobs and families that gave them some status in society. But they were let down by the people who should have been the ones they could rely on. Not that it was a guarantee; she'd also seen plenty who'd had opportunities as a child and thrown them away to take a darker path.

A bad upbringing also wasn't a guarantee of turning to crime: Saskia would like to think that she was an example of that. When David and she were younger, it had been the two of them against the world. Their mother had done the best she could, but ultimately, she was terrified of their father. Saskia always saw him for what he was, a broken man, a facsimile of a human being who was more machine than living person. Even at a very young age she'd had no illusion as to where she stood in her father's eyes.

When David was a little boy he'd been easier to control, but each passing year the monster inside of him grew. Had that little boy she'd sworn to protect now totally gone? Saskia felt a knot of fear inside. She'd spent her whole life trying to prevent David from becoming their father, but ultimately, was she fighting a losing battle?

SIXTEEN

Back at the office, Winter put two officers on the job of looking through every second of the security camera footage from La Hougue Bie. He looked through it too, keen to see how the drama had unfolded last night.

Everything seemed quiet until the alarm was tripped. The security guard came running out, and Winter saw him talking on his phone as he jogged around the site. Less than ten minutes later, the two honorary police arrived. How was it that they were so quick on the scene? Just over five minutes later and the two States of Jersey police officers drove up to the site. He watched as all five of them started wandering around the area with their torches, checking that nobody was there, no damage had been caused and nothing had been stolen. Then there was a gap in the footage. The time clock jumped nearly ten minutes and came back to them all still looking around the site. Had all five of them walked past the entrance to the dolmen? Did any of them go inside, or did they just shine their torches down the passageway? Winter had no way of knowing.

'Why's there a gap in the CCTV footage?' Winter asked Jonno.

'It doesn't record when someone is reviewing recorded footage and the security guard looked through to check to see if he could see anyone doing anything or hiding somewhere.'

'Did he... OK, I'd like to talk to him, and have we got hold of those two honoraries yet?' Winter shouted over to DC Sarah Fuller.

'One is working at a shop in town. Said his day off is tomorrow, he can pop into the station to see you on his way home. The other is retired and he's at home and available to talk from two p.m. today. The two uniforms, PCs Scott Askew and Matthew Drew, clocked off at six a.m. this morning so we haven't disturbed them as they'll be asleep, but should be OK to talk to them mid-afternoon.'

'OK set it up with all of them, would you? And do some background checks on each of them too.'

'You think one of them put the head there and is our killer?'

'It's a possibility we have to rule out,' Winter said pointedly. He knew his team felt uncomfortable about suspecting one of their own, but it had to be investigated.

There was some good background information on the two victims, Sandra and Barbara, and so Winter sent this on to Saskia. When lunchtime came and went, he headed out to see Alec Jeune, one of the honorary officers who had been first on the scene to help the security guard.

Alec had the door open and a big smile on his face before Winter had even got out of his car. It was obvious that he was enjoying being a part of a bigger investigation.

'Come in, Detective Inspector.' Alec waved him in.

'This is my colleague, Detective Constable Sarah Fuller,' Winter introduced her.

'This is my wife, Susan,' Alec introduced them to a woman who had come out of the kitchen with a big smile on her face. 'Would you both like a tea or coffee?'

'A coffee would be lovely, thank you,' Winter said.

'Milk and sugar?' Susan asked.

'Just milk thanks.'

Susan looked to Sarah.

'The same, thank you,' she'd replied smiling.

'Come on through to the sitting room. You're not allergic to cats I hope. Porthos and Aramis are somewhat housebound these days. They're both fifteen, which I'm told is eighty-five in human years so sadly they're not up to going outside and chasing birds and mice these days.'

Winter thought that the local bird and rodent population would not find that a sad piece of news at all. He'd read recently that cats in America kill over a billion birds each year, with fifty-five million a year in the UK, but according to the latest study, Australians say it's over a million a day. Either way, two less cats out catching sparrows and robins would no doubt be good for their survival. The two cats in question were lounging on a couple of chairs by the patio doors. Clearly watching their former prey through the windows was now far more pleasurable.

'How can I help you, detectives,' Alec said, settling down in a large wingback armchair and gesticulating for them to sit on the sofa opposite.

'You attended the alarm call at Hougue Bie last night,' Winter began. 'I wonder if you could first of all tell me how you came to be in the area and to be alerted?'

'Yes, yes, yes, of course,' Alec began enthusiastically. 'Michael and I had been out late seeing if we could catch a few lads who've been speeding along one of the roads nearby. We've had several complaints from parishioners that there seemed to be a regular meet up going on and potentially some road racing. We went out about half eleven and had just called it a night when the call came through about the alarm at Hougue Bie. It had unfortunately been a boring and frustrating night. The kids must have been tipped off that we were there and didn't turn up. So, we thought we'd assist at Hougue Bie. We were literally just a minute or two's drive away.'

'Had you seen anybody in the area prior to that? Were you logging vehicles?'

'We hadn't seen anyone for a while. Definitely nobody on foot. We'd both taken it in turns to walk around the area every now and then, just to be sure we weren't missing anything by sitting in the car. Nothing.'

The sitting room door opened. 'Here you go, two white coffees, and a tea for you, darling,' Susan addressed them all, taking the mugs off a tray as she worked her way around the room.

'Thank you, my love,' Alec replied, beaming at her.

Winter was looking for any signs of the kind of person that Saskia had talked about. Someone with a dysfunctional relationship with an older woman. Alec and Susan seemed to be happy and content with each other, although it wouldn't be the first time that he'd met an individual in a coercive relationship who always had a smile on their face in public. It was part of their survival technique. The abusers themselves were always charming and seemingly loving and attentive in front of people too. You had to look for the smaller, more subtle clues beyond the smiles and loving words.

'What did you find when you arrived at the site?' Winter continued.

'Marek, the security guard, had already done a quick jog around the site and said he'd seen nothing. We decided to be more systematic and check everywhere thoroughly.'

'Do you know at what point he decided to take a look through the CCTV?'

'I'm not sure exactly. He didn't mention that to us.'

'Did you spot anything when you looked around, anything at all suspicious?'

Alec shook his head. 'We didn't see anyone or anything untoward.'

'I have to ask you about the dolmen itself. Did you go inside the chamber?'

'Not inside as such, no.' Alec looked somewhat concerned at this question, as though he'd been found with his hand in the cookie jar. He put his mug down on the little table beside his chair, the relaxed pose gone. 'We looked really thoroughly, shone the torches into the chamber and didn't see anyone at all. It's only narrow, there's no way anyone could have hidden.'

'Were you aware of the final chamber with the standing stones at the end? It's possible that someone could have been hiding in there and you wouldn't have seen them from the entrance.'

'No,' Alec replied, sounding dejected.

'Did you see the two States police officers arrive?' Winter changed the subject, aware that Alec was losing his enthusiasm for the interview.

'We saw them blue lighting past us as we headed up the mound to the little chapel, and then met up with them as we were all looking around.'

'Did you all stick to searching in pairs?'

'Mostly, but occasionally we split up if one was looking at something in particular or thought they may have seen something.'

'Tell me about your partner,' Winter asked.

'Michael?' Alec said surprised. 'He's a damned good lad, he is. Been with us for about three years now. Trustworthy, always on time. Never known him to let us down on a shift.'

'Are you aware of what we have found in the dolmen passageway?'

'I've heard rumours of a body. I can tell you there was no body in there when we looked.'

'It isn't a body, Mr Jeune, it's a severed head.'

Alec's eyes widened and he took a sharp intake of breath.

'I'd like to ask you not to repeat that please, for obvious reasons,' Winter added.

'There's no way that was in there when we looked. How far in was it?'

'About two thirds of the way.'

'Good Lord. I'm sorry, detective, but I can't help you with that. We certainly didn't see it. It was definitely not there when we looked.'

'And you looked together?'

'Yes, we looked together, both of us took it in turns to crouch down and shine our torches in.'

Winter asked a few more questions, focusing on what Alec had seen the other people present doing, but as soon as their coffees were drunk, he said thank you to the Jeunes and they left.

'Well, that wasn't much help,' DC Fuller said to him as they got back in the car.

'Not a great deal, no, although it confirms that the two honoraries didn't enter the chamber so would have struggled to see the head. If the other two did the same then that gives us the possibility that the killer got in, threw in the head and was gone again before they'd even started to search. The killer could have even been hiding in the end chamber cell.' Winter sighed. 'Just got to hope forensics turn something up at Sandra Cunningham's house.'

SEVENTEEN

Saskia had only been home ten minutes when she saw headlights pull up outside her cottage and then the accompanying bark of her next-door neighbour June's dog, Pushki. She opened her front door to find David glaring over the boundary wall at the little animal.

'David, sorry did I miss a text?' Saskia asked, surprised.

'Why do you keep texting me?' He growled as he walked past her on the doorstep and into her cottage.

She bit her tongue. Rising to his aggression would not do her any favours. 'Do you want a drink? I've just got in.'

'No. I'm here like you asked me to come. I want you to stop texting. It's annoying.'

'Annoying? Are you OK?' Saskia studied him, looking for any signs that he was beginning to lose his self-control. David was a good-looking guy, and his appearance as usual was impeccable. There was no emotion on his face; his eyes were as dead as they usually were when he looked at her.

'I'm fine. Why do you keep texting?'

'You missed our session and I hadn't heard back from you so

I was concerned. You know why we hold these meetings. Has something happened?'

David looked at her, his eyes staring into hers. Locked on. Cold dark beams of focus.

'Nothing's happened. Things are good. I'm not sure these meetings are necessary anymore. I'm fine. I'm happy.'

'That's not our deal, David,' Saskia said tentatively. Her heart was starting to race. She could feel a shift in his attitude.

'I've got Jackie now, I don't need you,' he replied, his expression not changing.

If David had been a non-psychopathic brother then Saskia would have agreed with that, but he wasn't. She knew what he might be capable of and their deal ensured that she could monitor him so he didn't break any of the basic rules of society. But how should she play this? If she argued with him then it could become confrontational. She needed to tease things out of him.

'How is Jackie?'

'She's OK. Been getting a bit forgetful lately and is tired all the time. But she's fine. I'm looking after her.'

'Really? I mean, she's a smart woman, her business is doing well.'

'Yeah well, I think she might be getting early dementia. Her mother has Alzheimer's, you know.'

'That must be hard for you,' Saskia tried the sympathy route.

'Yeah, it is. Like hanging out with your ageing parent if I'm honest, but you know, she might not be around that much longer if she carries on like this. We're already talking about me helping her more with the business and becoming a co-signatory on the house so that if she becomes incapacitated, I can help.'

Saskia tried not to rise to it, but the way David had just said that, it sounded more like a threat than a regretful statement.

'Is she OK after what happened to Allan and her necklace being stolen?'

'She's fine.'

'You thought anymore about giving the necklace back? You could easily find it somewhere in the garage.'

David frowned again, although with his Botox, it means his forehead barely wrinkled. 'I really don't think that a fifty grand necklace matters to her now, but it's a little safety net for me, if I need it. You have got it safe, haven't you?'

'I have.'

'Where is it?' David asked, his eyes narrowing slightly.

'Not here. I've buried it somewhere.'

'Where? You need to tell me where in case I need it.'

'I will. When and if you need it.'

There was a tense silence between the two of them for a few moments. Saskia was taken back to when they were teenagers. It was a year or so after David had attacked the boy at school who'd bullied her. Their dad had been out of their lives for a few years and their mother was always working, trying to pay the bills. Usually she'd work nights and Saskia would have to mind David. He'd grown increasingly difficult to manage. Refusing to stay in and disappearing out for hours on end. One particular night, he'd shoved her out the way when she'd tried to persuade him not to leave, and gone out in a raging mood. Teenage hormones combined with his psychopathy had turned him into an unpredictable time bomb. An hour later, he'd come home and there was blood on his clothes.

'What have you done?' she'd asked him. *'Are you hurt?'*

He'd shrugged and gone to take a shower. While he was in the bathroom, Saskia had gone into protection mode. Deep down, she knew that if the blood wasn't his then he'd been involved in something which could come back and bite him big time. She'd taken his clothes and his trainers, put them in a bag and walked them down to the communal rubbish bins on the ground floor. She'd been just about to put them in, when a thought had crossed her mind that the police, if they came, might think to look in them. So, instead, she'd run across the street and dumped the carrier bag into the pub's bins, making sure to bury it under some other waste. She had no idea what had happened, but her first instinct was to protect him. By the time she got back to the flat, David had finished and was lounging on the sofa in front of the TV as though nothing had happened. Saskia went and stood in between him and the TV screen.

'What happened?' she'd asked him, arms folded.

'Get out the way,' he'd replied defiantly.

'Not until you tell me what happened.'

'Nothing, now get out the way.'

At that moment the doorbell to their flat had gone, and there was a knock, *'Police, can you open up please.'*

David had looked at her without one iota of panic or fear. It was Saskia who felt the panic. She'd gone to the door and let in three police officers, two male and one female.

'David Carter in?'

'Yeah, he's been in since he came home from school. Why?'

The police officer had looked at her with a penetrating gaze.

'We have reason to believe he's just stabbed someone outside of the High Kent pub.'

'Well that's impossible, he's only fourteen and has been in all evening.' Saskia knew the pub they were talking about. It wasn't the one near to the flats, it was a rough dive a few streets away.

The three police officers walked into the sitting room where David was still lounging in front of the TV, taking no notice of the conversation that was taking place.

'David Carter?' the older male police officer had asked.

'Yeah,' David had replied looking up at him.

'We have two witnesses who say that you were arguing with

Liam Watson earlier this evening, and that you stabbed him seven times with a knife.'

'Where would I get a knife from?' David asked, cool as a cucumber.

Saskia found it almost chilling to see how calm he was in the face of three police officers accusing him of a serious crime.

'The knife allegedly belonged to the victim.'

David shrugged. *'Nothing to do with me, I've been here all night and if it was his knife then why aren't you asking him? He's a right nasty git, if someone stabbed him then he probably deserved it.'*

'His girlfriend says that you and she had been in a brief relationship and Watson found out. When he confronted you, you took his knife off him and stabbed him.'

'I'm fourteen, what kind of relationship do you mean?'

'Where's your mother?' This question was directed at Saskia.

'She's working. We're OK here on our own, I'm fifteen. We had dinner and we started watching TV. How can you accuse a fourteen-year-old of something like this?'

'Believe me, it wouldn't be the first time. Do you mind if we look around? You been in those clothes all night?'

'Yeah, and yeah. I've got nothing to hide, but do you have a warrant?' David asked.

Saskia was shocked by how defiant he seemed. She tried to diffuse the situation.

'Look, we seriously don't have anything to hide. We've been here together all evening. He's a fourteen-year-old school kid, are you sure you've got the right person?'

'He was witnessed as wearing black trainers, a black T-shirt and jeans. We have enough reason to seize those items.' The officer continued. *'Are you going to show me where his room is?'*

Saskia had taken them through to David's bedroom, safe in the knowledge that she'd already disposed of the clothes.

'Trainers?' the officer had asked. Saskia had pointed to David's spare trainers, which were chucked at the bottom of his wardrobe.

The female police officer had immediately gone to the pile of worn clothing on the floor and pulled out a pair of jeans and a black T-shirt. Saskia praised the fact that when David liked a style, he stuck to it. He had several black T-shirts and a few pairs of jeans, along with the two pairs of black trainers. The police left their flat that night happy that they'd seized the clothing he'd worn earlier. Saskia knew that without any evidence, the case would never stand.

Over the years, Saskia had excused her moral self for what she did that night by telling herself that Liam Watson, the man David stabbed, was a bad person. He was known for carrying a knife and being aggressive. His girlfriend usually sported a black eye or a bruise of some kind. What David thought he was doing, Saskia didn't know, but she suspected it was to goad Watson. Liam was in hospital for weeks after the attack and never fully recovered. He didn't bully his girlfriends or anyone else again, and that, Saskia rationalised, had been a good outcome.

Now, assessing David as a grown man, Saskia realised he was far more dangerous than the adolescent fourteen-year-old boy. He was smart, sexually mature, and he was manipulative. The teen aggression of his early years had given way to subtle control that she knew full well had the potential to be deadly. Saskia also realised something else. She had spent her life hating her father. The man who was incapable of love, the serial killer who murdered a string of women and nearly strangled her own mother too.

As she looked at David, she realised that he was everything her father was but with a more sophisticated veneer. There was nothing about him that she could love. No ounce of human spirit that engendered compassion or sisterly devotion. She had protected him and guided him her whole life out of a sense of duty and at the expense of her own life's experiences. Now, she felt he was on the cusp of hurting someone. Jackie could well be in danger and Saskia knew that she was the only person who could save her, even if it meant betraying her brother and coming clean about her own relationship to David and their father.

EIGHTEEN

PC Scott Askew came to find Winter the minute he'd reported for duty that afternoon.

'I understand you want to talk to me about last night's call-out at Hougue Bie,' he said to Winter.

Scott was mid-thirties but with a young face that meant he could probably pass for late twenties to early thirties. He reminded Winter of Ben Shephard, the British TV presenter, in looks. *Tipping Point* had been one of his favourite quiz shows when he'd been a young detective and managed to get home before the six o'clock news.

'Yes, thanks for coming up. I've read your statement, but just wanted to go over a few things with you.'

'Absolutely, sir.'

'Can you just talk me through the scene, as it was when you arrived? Who was there and where?'

'Right, so the honoraries had got there before us and Marek, the security guy, had said they'd started off going clockwise round the site. We could see their torches over where the longhouse is. Matt and I decided to follow their route, double-check everything.'

'What was your first impression of Marek?'

Scott pulled his mouth into a thoughtful grimace. 'He was worried. They'd not had the alarms go off before and I think it had given him a bit of a turn. You know some of these security jobs are easy, right? The most they have to deal with is the odd drunk or bunch of kids. He couldn't understand what it was that had tripped the alarm and that seemed to be bothering him.'

'So, how did you decide to conduct your search?'

'You think we didn't look properly because the head's been found?' Scott took a defensive stance.

'I'm not in the blame game. By all accounts, the head would have been very difficult to spot from the entrance as it had rolled mostly behind one of the standing stones. The tourist who found it didn't see it until he was right on top of it.'

Scott relaxed a little, but Winter could sense he was still on edge.

'Right, sorry, sir. I was just... well, you know it was a bit of a shock to hear about the head. Feel like we might be accused of not doing our jobs right. Thing is, I did go part way into that passage grave. I know from visiting the place as a kid that there's a section at the end about the size of a shower cubicle, where someone could hide. I went most of the way down towards that and saw nothing. That head wasn't in there, I'm telling you. There's no way I could have missed it.'

'How far down did you go? I'm not being judgemental, just want to get the facts and the timeline straight. If you didn't see the head and you had got to the section where we found it, then it didn't get put in there until after you'd left. That's pretty important.'

Winter pulled up some of the forensic photographs on his screen.

'Take a look at these images of the tunnel. This one is from the entrance, you can see straight down to the end, but you can't really see the head.' Winter clicked on a couple of images. 'This one is halfway. Did you get this far?'

'Yes, I went past that, to here.' Askew pointed to an area of the chamber on the screen. But I can see the head from this photograph. I'm a hundred per cent sure that wasn't there when I went in.'

'You obviously had a torch, you'd have been searching around.'

'Yeah, yeah. Look, sir, I'll be honest. The place is a little bit creepy in the dead of night. I was looking everywhere to see if someone or something was in there, but I was also scanning everything because it made me feel a little uneasy. Know what I mean?'

'Yes, I can imagine. Is that why you didn't go all the way in?'

Scott grimaced again. Winter could see he didn't want to admit to being scared of the place. 'I could see the place was empty. I reached a spot where I could stand up, was happy there was nobody in there and left. I would have seen that head if it had been there then.'

'At what point did you go into the dolmen? Was it your first search area?'

'Like I said, we went clockwise, so our first search was the museum. We were thorough, so we were about ten minutes checking all round the building. It was secure, nobody was in there. Then we moved on to the dolmen.'

'And where were the honorary officers and Marek at that point?'

Scott narrowed his eyes in thought. 'There were voices back at the car park area, so I think they'd finished their search and were all talking there. But we were round the side of the mound by this time, so it's feasible that somebody could have been on the other side and we couldn't see them.'

Winter nodded thoughtfully. 'Do you know if anyone else

went round the back of the mound again, near the dolmen entrance, after you'd searched it?'

'I couldn't say, sir. We went up to the chapel after the passage grave, and then came down and checked around the rest of the grounds. The honoraries had definitely finished by the time we came back to the car park and Marek had been scanning through the CCTV to see if he'd missed anyone setting off the alarms. We all agreed that it was probably a false alarm, and us and the honoraries left.'

'You all left together?'

'Yeah, apart from Marek obviously. The honoraries left first and then when we drove out, Marek closed the gate behind us.'

'OK, thank you, and there's nothing else that comes to mind? No noises or something you found unusual?'

'No. We'd have investigated it. I saw nothing and heard nothing unusual. The site was empty and that head was not in the passage grave.'

'OK. Thank you.'

'That it, sir?'

'For now, yes.'

PC Askew headed out the office, just as his partner from the previous night, PC Matthew Drew was walking in. Winter watched as they gave each other a high five and spoke briefly. He saw Drew glance over at him and then they both parted company.

'Detective Inspector Labey?' PC Drew walked up to his desk.

'Yes, please take a seat.' He indicated the chair that just a few minutes earlier Scott had been sitting in. Matthew was bigger than his partner. Over six feet in height and with a thick, neatly trimmed beard that made him look a little older than his thirty-two years. He wasn't as nervous as Scott; Winter judged him to have a confidence that came with being well-built and knowing just his stature could be intimidating.

'As I said to your colleague, I've read your reports, but I'm just trying to get a good grasp on the timeline of events last night. So, could you tell me what you found when you arrived at the Hougue Bie site?'

PC Drew recounted the same story as Askew.

'Did you go into the passage grave?'

'No, left that to Scott. I'd looked in there with my torch, and seen nothing, but he reckoned there was a section at the back where it might be possible for someone to hide. He wasn't keen about going in–' Matthew allowed himself a small smirk at this point – 'but I reminded him that he'd volunteered himself and is about a foot shorter than me, so would find it easier.'

'Did you stay at the entrance?'

'Yeah. I kept my torch on the passageway and stayed watching him. If there was someone hiding in there who wasn't friendly then I needed to be ready to back him up.'

'I've got some photographs of the passageway and the chamber, could you show me how far you think he got to before turning around?'

PC Drew pointed to roughly the same area as Askew had.

'And obviously, neither of you saw a head lying on the ground,' Winter asked unnecessarily, but wanted to see his reaction.

'No. Absolutely not. Scott would definitely have seen it and I saw nothing from where I was.'

'Did you notice if anyone else went back to the passage grave after you'd carried on your search?'

'It was dark round that side so someone would have had to use a torch and I didn't notice one going in that direction. If they didn't use a light then maybe we just wouldn't have seen them at all. Both the honoraries and Marek the security guy were in the car park area when we finished though. I can't account for their full whereabouts while we were searching the site, but I didn't see anyone going round to the entranceway after we'd searched it.'

Winter was frustrated by the interviews. From what he could see, the killer couldn't have deposited the head in the burial chamber until after all the police had searched it, and yet there was nothing caught on camera. The big question mark was what happened in the time after PC Askew had exited the dolmen, to when they all left. The camera wasn't recording. All four police officers were searching the site and Marek was looking at the CCTV recordings, so could someone have crept back and thrown the head in then?

He asked the team to find all the CCTV in the area to see if they could track down any cars which hadn't been accounted for. He also ordered up the full background checks and employment records of the two police constables, the two honorary officers, and the security guard, Marek Dubanowski. Tomorrow he'd speak to the second of the two honoraries, Michael Rault, and see if his story matched up to the others. Plus, he'd asked to see Marek Dubanowski. By searching the CCTV footage, he'd stopped the cameras recording. Was that deliberate or accidental?

It had been a frustrating day from the point of view of the inquiry, and Winter was keen to make progress. At some point during the afternoon he'd made up his mind to go and speak to Saskia to clear the air and tell her how he felt about what happened and their relationship. He knew that it was playing on his mind and that wasn't good for his concentration. Once he'd decided to go, he found himself to be in a bullish mood, ready to deal with the situation and hopeful that by this evening, he and Saskia would be back on track. If he couldn't sort the day job out, he was going to sort out his love life – or rather, lack of it.

Winter's excuse to see Saskia was that he now had a photofit of the man who neighbours had seen visiting Barbara Smith's house. She'd indicated in her email reply earlier that she was almost ready with the profile and so Winter calculated that this evening would be a good time to chat it through.

He toyed with the idea of calling her first. He certainly would usually, but he didn't want her to give him a lame excuse because she was still avoiding him. If he just turned up then it would be a lot harder for her to turn him away. Of course, he could be running the risk that she wasn't going to be in, but at this point in Winter's mindset, that was most definitely worth the risk. En route he picked up a bottle of wine, some crisps, and a couple of luxury ready meals, just in case.

As Winter pulled up outside of Saskia's cottage, he could see that the lights were on in her kitchen and sitting room. She was in. He went to pick up the wine and food, but hesitated. Maybe that looked a bit presumptuous. He'd leave them in the car until they'd at least managed to clear the air. He gathered up some paperwork and his laptop and marched to her front door, anticipation and nerves jostling at his insides.

He knocked. Was that voices he heard inside?

Nothing.

He knocked again and the door was opened. Saskia peered around the edge of the door and looked shocked and a little panicked when she saw him.

'Detective Labey,' she said, 'I wasn't expecting you.'

'I know, my apologies, but I was in the area and thought I'd catch up on a few things with the investigation,' he fibbed. It was only a little white lie and for a good cause. 'I also wanted to talk to you anyway,' he continued.

'Right,' she looked decidedly flustered now and didn't open the door fully, keeping him on the doorstep. 'It's not a great time,' she said to him.

He knew she was upset with him, but this seemed like

something else. 'Is everything OK, Saskia? I mean I know you're a little upset with me. I apologise about the text—'

'No, it's fine. Let's talk in the morning. Can we?' She definitely looked slightly panicked as though she wanted to get rid of him quickly. He'd never seen her like this before.

'Are you sure you're OK?' he asked again, worried that perhaps someone was inside threatening her.

'I am absolutely fine, thank you. It's just now is not a good time, so I'll speak to you in the morning.'

'OK,' Winter replied because he didn't know what else to say. He backed down off the front doorstep and watched as she closed the door.

He was left standing outside in her garden in silence.

Well that didn't go to plan, he muttered to himself.

He heard a man's voice inside the cottage again. Saskia had somebody in there with her. This is what he'd feared all the way along: that she had another man, that it was complicated and she couldn't commit. It would explain so much. He felt like he'd just gone up in a lift too fast and left his stomach behind on the ground floor.

Winter walked back to his car and dumped everything onto the passenger seat. He stared at her cottage and looked down the lane. He hadn't seen it when he first arrived, but parked further down was a black BMW, hidden in the shadows.

A large glass of whisky appeared in Winter's head and he was about to turn on the ignition to drive home and down one, when Saskia's front garden was lit up by the front door opening.

'We're done, Saskia,' a handsome dark-haired man was saying over his shoulder as he strode through the door and down the path.

Winter knew that face. He racked his brain, working through the hundreds of people that he'd spoken to in recent weeks and months. Then, he remembered. David Carter, the partner of Jackie Slater whose driver had been murdered. Why was he here with Saskia? Had they been having an affair? It would explain why Saskia had been so worried about him being there. Although, from what David had just said, it sounded like he'd just dumped her.

Winter turned his ignition and headlights on and pulled away. As he drove past, he gave one last glance to Saskia's cottage. She was standing watching him, a horrified look on her face.

His mind went into overdrive all the way home. She was obviously so panicked because she realised that he now knew about her and David. She'd never once mentioned him when they'd talked about Allan Hall's murder and she'd never once said that she was seeing someone else. All this time he'd been worrying that he'd upset her by not being clearer with his feelings after that kiss, and she was the one who had secrets and wasn't available. He felt like a fool, but most of all he felt gut-wrenchingly disappointed. He'd been so confident that tonight they would sort things out, he'd clear his head, and now it was a hundred times worse.

His phone buzzed to say he'd received a couple of text messages. He longed to look at them, but apart from the fact he was driving and couldn't, he also didn't want to. It was childish, but he wanted to give her the cold shoulder, even if it was for just a few minutes until he reached home.

It was literally as he was parking up that his phone rang. If it had been Saskia he wasn't sure if he was going to answer it, but as it was, it was his mother. He was in no mood to chat with her right now; not through any fault of hers, but because his head was about to explode. He yanked the bag of food and wine out of the car, along with his work stuff and stomped up the stairs to his flat.

His phone buzzed again and he saw his mother's name come up on WhatsApp. She'd messaged him. He'd read it later.

His priority was a large glass of Scotch and then he'd read what Saskia had to say about what had just happened.

He poured the amber liquid over some ice and took a big sip. Now he was ready to read Saskia's text message.

> So sorry about earlier. I had a client session. It was awkward.

A client session? Since when did she take private clients? Now she was definitely lying to him. He didn't know what to say back. He had no right to be annoyed with her; they weren't an item and yet he was behaving and feeling as though he'd just been cheated on. He couldn't say that to her, he couldn't tell her how he was feeling. Instead he reverted to type.

> No worries. We can talk in the morning about the case. Was hoping to go through the dolmen killer profile. If you can come to the station tomorrow morning that would be good.

He read and reread the text several times, pressed send, and downed the rest of his whisky. He couldn't compete with the good looks of David Carter. The man was as smooth as ice and probably had at least twice or three times the bank balance.

Whatever had possessed Winter to think that he could have Saskia Monet? He poured another whisky and paced up and down the living room in his flat, drinking it. He felt as though some kind of amphetamine was pumping around his bloodstream, confusing him, making him emotional, raising his blood pressure, encouraging his testosterone to fight. He knocked back his second glass of whisky to try to dampen the effect, but it didn't help, so he poured a third. Finally, as the alcohol seeped into his brain, he began to feel tired. He stumbled into the bathroom and bedroom, bouncing off the doorframe in his slightly drunken exhaustion, and collapsed into bed. All he wanted was to turn his back on a shit day and forget how he felt right now about Saskia Monet.

NINETEEN

She always ruined it. No matter what he did for her, no matter how good a son he was, she always turned on him.

He'd gone back round to Mrs Baxter's house that evening. She'd been surprised to see him, but she invited him in and made him a cup of tea.

'I'm sorry I don't have any biscuits, I wasn't expecting you,' she'd said to him. 'Maybe next time you can text me to say you'll be coming round.'

She'd glanced at the TV then; it was frozen. Paused on some TV programme that he didn't recognise. Even at that point it was obvious that she'd rather be watching the television than talking to him.

He'd told her about his day and she'd been pleasant enough, as though she was interested in what he was saying, but he could see her eyes kept wandering back to the television and so he'd asked her what she'd been watching.

'It's a drama series,' she'd said. 'This is the last episode, it's been really good.'

He'd nodded politely.

'I don't mind if you watch it,' he'd said to her then.

She seemed to brighten and she'd smiled at him.

'Oh, do you mind, thank you. I'll see you out and you're welcome to come back next week.'

'I meant I could sit here with you and watch it,' he'd said to her then. Upset that she seemed as though she didn't want him to be there. 'Do you not like me visiting? I thought you liked me coming around.'

Her face had changed then. The smile disappeared, wiped out by a look he'd seen before. She looked a little frightened. Her eyes scrutinised him as though seeing him for the first time.

'Of course I enjoy your visits,' she'd said, 'it's just that it's a little late for me. I'm going to be going to bed as soon as I've watched this. I'm tired.'

He knew how to read between the lines.

'Sorry to have kept you up,' he said to her, smiling. 'I'll see myself out, don't you worry.'

She'd perked up a bit then, the smile returning. He knew it was a smile of betrayal. One that was glad to see him go, not pleased with him. But he couldn't help himself. He still wanted her love.

'Light working OK?' he'd asked as he was going.

'Oh yes, all good. Thank you again for doing that for me,' she'd said to him, looking up from her armchair. As he walked out the room, he saw she'd already got the remote control again ready to press play on the paused TV.

On his way through the hall, he'd quietly picked up the spare key that she kept by the front door. He'd come back later when she could give him her undivided attention.

TWENTY

Saskia was nearly sick after she'd closed the front door to David and Winter. The one thing she'd been fearing for months, and now Winter knew she had a connection to David, and he probably thought it was a romantic one. The situation with Winter had been solved in one simple act. She either had to go along with his assumption and never again contemplate any kind of relationship with him, or she had to come clean, which would in theory clear the way for her and Winter to have a proper relationship, but in practice would almost certainly mean that he would be repulsed by her family history and wouldn't trust her ever again. Either way, it was a lose-lose situation for her.

If that was her only problem then it would have been enough to deal with, but it wasn't. She and David had been arguing when Winter knocked. His parting words were that he wasn't going to come to any more sessions; there was nothing wrong with him and he didn't want her interfering in his life anymore. That posed her a far greater problem.

Up until now she'd been David's ally, supporting him and helping him to maintain his role in society. If she was right, and every element of her training – and more importantly her lived experience – told her she was, then Jackie could be in danger. David had intimated as much in what he'd said about his ambitions. Saskia had sworn a vow to herself that she would never stand by and allow her psychopathic family to create another victim – not knowingly. It was why she was here in Jersey monitoring her brother. It was why they had their agreement that he come to sessions where she could assess him and remind him of how society expected him to behave.

She knew David was only with Jackie because of her money, but that wasn't a crime she could damn him for. There were plenty of people who weren't psychopaths who chose partners based on wealth and status – that had been going on for centuries. What was concerning was the fact that David was clearly contemplating a life without Jackie but with her house and money. As she was a fit healthy woman, that meant only one thing.

If Saskia did what she was thinking about doing – went to Jackie and told her she might be in danger – then she would instantly become enemy number one for David. She knew how much he hated their mother after she'd tried to get him diagnosed and put into care all those years ago. Their mother had failed, David had been too smart for the tests, but it meant he vowed to finish off the job that his father had started, and kill her. Saskia knew that by saving Jackie she could be putting her own life at risk.

After the initial shock of the two men in her life being in the same place at the same time, Saskia had got herself a glass of water and gone to sit down in her sitting room. The look of hurt and shock on Winter's face was indelibly scored onto the back of her eyelids, so she texted him. There was so much she wanted to say, but she said none of it. Instead she made up a feeble excuse. She couldn't bear the thought of how he would look at her knowing where she'd come from, and so she'd lied.

After that, a quiet calm had come over her. She knew what

she had to do and so that's exactly what she would do. There was no room for emotion or misplaced family loyalty; she switched into professional mode. Her fears over David's propensity to harm had been rising and although she'd tried to ignore them and double-down on his therapy, she knew in her heart that she couldn't change his nature.

Saskia did what she always did in life. She sealed her heart shut to the pain of her reality. There were no tears, no drama. She didn't feel anything about the prospect of betraying her brother. It was a protection mechanism, she knew that, but when she felt like this her other fear came into play. That she too could have inherited the psychopathy curse of her family. That she was incapable of love and feeling the deep emotions that other warm human beings felt. So she turned on the film *Hachi: A Dog's Tale*, and allowed herself to cry. For the dog and his devotion to the man he loved. For the passing of the years while he waited for the man he loved to return. A pain that would never end. A sadness that could never be appeased, even by the friendships of those around him.

Warm, salty tears flowed down Saskia's cheeks and showed her that she wasn't a cold reptile inside like her brother and her father. That she could appreciate love and the value of life.

Tomorrow she would do what she had to do.

TWENTY-ONE
THURSDAY

Saskia woke early, aware that she'd tossed and turned in the night, black thoughts pulling her from rest. It was still dark and so she'd gone downstairs and sat with her laptop in the kitchen having her breakfast. Winter had texted her and asked if she could come into the station that morning to talk through the case and her profile, but there was no way she felt strong enough to face up to him just yet, and besides she had work meetings. She declined but said she'd be back in touch with the full profile shortly.

She got quite a few work emails done as she finished her porridge, and then did some more work on the profile report that she'd started to put together for Winter and the team. By the time she'd done that, the day had begun and so she took a shower and headed into work.

At about eleven a.m. she phoned Jackie Slater. She told her she was looking to invest in some property after coming into some family money and that her name was Alice Moody. They arranged to meet the following morning.

After she'd put the phone down, Saskia stared at it for a few minutes, questioning if she was doing the right thing. What if she was wrong? What if David had really mellowed and he and Jackie were happy? What if she was about to ruin everything just because her own imagination had overrun? But then the professional psychiatrist in her had taken back control. If David wasn't her brother, she'd have already flagged up the warning signs she'd been seeing. She didn't want blood on her conscience and if she didn't warn Jackie, that's exactly what could happen. David had broken the unwritten terms of their relationship and said he no longer wanted her in his life, that he didn't need their sessions. That was reason enough.

It was a mostly uneventful day of meetings and assessments, but Saskia berated herself for staying in her office as much as possible. She knew why it was: she didn't want to bump into Mark Byrne and that was ridiculous. She couldn't allow him to bully her. To drive the point home, in the afternoon she'd gone to the wing where she knew he worked, in order to interview a prisoner. Saskia had kicked herself mentally when, on discovering Mark Byrne wasn't there, she'd felt her shoulder drop and a big sigh of relief escape her. A casual question to one of the guards on duty and she was told that he'd taken one of the prisoners to a meeting with the parole team. She'd just missed him. At least something was going right for her.

When she got back to her office, another email had come through from Winter. This one contained the photofit of the man who the neighbours had seen visiting Barbara Smith's house. She clicked on the attachment, wondering if it resembled the man she'd been developing the profile for. When she saw the image come up on her screen, it made her gasp out loud. A big man with a dark beard. It could have been a photofit of Mark Byrne.

She knew these composite images were always a little off the mark. Witness memories weren't the most reliable and it could be a whole different skill set in itself to translate the memory in your head into an image. This man definitely had black hair and a black beard, just like Mark. He did look a little younger and maybe not so overweight, but there was no getting away from the fact that in his black prison guard uniform, he bore more than just a passing resemblance. The uniform could easily be mistaken for a police uniform to someone who didn't know the difference and especially if they'd seen him in the dark.

Saskia knew Mark had psychopathic tendencies, he was a bully who didn't seem to care about anyone, and she also knew that he lived at home with his mother still. She'd been convinced that the person behind the murders wasn't necessarily psychopathic. She'd found his choice of burial sites contradicted with a person who cared nothing for society's rules or an individual's best interests. But, maybe she was wrong. She'd had a lot on her mind lately with David and even the situation with Winter. Was her clinical judgement impaired? Could the killer be right under her nose? Could Mark Byrne be the dolmen murderer?

TWENTY-TWO

Winter woke up with a slight headache, which wasn't totally unexpected bearing in mind the three very large glasses of whisky that he'd downed before bed. He felt crap in more ways than one. Bloody David Carter was having his cake and eating it. He thought Saskia would have had better taste than just to go for his good looks.

He looked at his phone and realised he hadn't read the text from his mum.

> Got an odd text from Enid, tonight. Tried calling her back but no reply. Might need your help.

He wasn't entirely sure if it was technical help his mother needed, or help with trying to track Enid down, but she was probably worrying about nothing. They'd been friends since school; he could remember countless occasions that Enid and her late husband Harold had been round to their house for dinner, or they'd gone to the beach for barbecues when he was much younger. Harold had unfortunately succumbed to cancer a decade ago, but Enid was a regular fixture in their house or her mother in hers. He'd give his mum a ring later to see if she'd managed to get hold of her friend. For now, he needed to get on with his job and try to forget about Saskia Monet.

Arriving at the office, Winter was greeted by the news that the La Hougue Bie head had been confirmed as that belonging to Sandra Cunningham. He wasn't particularly surprised by that news. He checked to find out how the tourist was getting on – he was due to be discharged later that morning, which was good news. Winter doubted the man would be able to tell him anything of use to the inquiry, but at least he wasn't going to suffer any long-term damage apart from nightmares.

The rest of the focus was on tracking vehicles which had been seen around the three sites: the two victims' homes and Hougue Bie. They cross-referenced all of them, seeing if there was a common denominator. So far that had drawn a blank. There was also a lot of work on the forensics side in both victims' homes. Several DNA profiles had been found in both, besides the victims', and the team were trying to isolate and identify all they could.

Winter had emailed the photofit of the suspect seen around Barbara Smith's house, to Saskia. He'd wanted to give it to her last night as it was already in the media this morning but at least he'd get it to her to help with the profile now. He also asked her how the profile was getting on. Right now they could do with any help they could get with leads. He couldn't let his personal feelings get in the way of his professional needs.

Just after lunch, the last of the two honorary police officers, Michael Rault, came into the station as he'd promised. The honoraries were volunteers, elected within their parishes and used for the more minor policing duties. Often they were retired people like Alec Jeune, keen to help their community, but Michael Rault was a younger man.

Winter was in a post-lunch slump, last night catching up on him, but he went down to reception to meet Michael. He was a quiet, unassuming character, very polite too. He'd said thank you and sorry to Winter at least half a dozen times before they sat down in the interview room. Aged in his forties, with dark hair, he had soft hazel eyes that watched Winter warily as though he was a feral dog afraid of a new master.

'Thank you for coming in,' Winter had said to him. 'I spoke to Alec Jeune yesterday. We're just trying to get an idea of the events at La Hougue Bie the night before last. I understand you and Alec arrived first, can you tell me how you came to be there?'

Winter was a little taken aback when Michael took a small notebook out of his pocket.

'Well, we weren't strictly first. The security guard, Marek Dubanowski, was already on site,' he said referring to his notes. 'We had been patrolling, looking for a group that's been racing around the back roads, and we'd just decided we were going to call it a day. We were so close to Hougue Bie that it took us less than five minutes to arrive after we'd heard the call. Mr Dubanowski opened the entrance gate for us and said that he was concerned somebody was on site because the alarms had been tripped. So, we started looking.'

'OK, and where did you search first?'

'We were systematic. We went clockwise, double-checking that the museum and visitor centre was locked up and then to the dolmen.'

'Did you go into the dolmen?'

Michael shook his head and pulled his eyebrows together. 'No. We shone our torches inside, there was nobody in there.'

'Are you aware of the chamber at the back?'

Michael's eyebrows came together and he shook his head.

'OK. Then where did you go after that?'

'We went up to the little chapel and then back down to the rest of the site. But the States police officers had arrived by then and were also looking around. I saw their torches near to the dolmen entrance.'

Michael's voice was quite soporific and Winter found himself struggling to focus.

'Did you go back and check the dolmen again at any point?'

Michael frowned and looked at Winter. 'No. We had looked everywhere and found nothing.'

'You are aware that partial human remains were found inside the burial chamber, in the morning?'

'Yes. But we didn't see anything. They weren't there when we looked. The passageway was empty.'

'Did you see the site security guard, Marek, checking the CCTV when you had finished your look around?'

'Yes, we thought that would be a good idea. If somebody had been there we'd see where they went.'

'And did you see anybody on the footage?'

'No,' he replied warily.

'OK, thank you. I'm not laying any blame, please don't think I am, we are just trying to work out the time frames.'

Michael had given a small smile at this, but didn't say anything further.

'Is there anything else you'd like to add?'

He shook his head.

'Well, thank you for coming in, Mr Rault,' Winter said.

When Winter got back to the office, he headed straight over to DC Peter Edwards.

'Pete, I'm not convinced about this Hougue Bie situation. There were five men there that night who saw nothing, but equally, there were five men there who had opportunity to put the victim's head in that chamber themselves. I need you to go through all that we have on them again. Re-check everything. I want to know their home lives, their professional records, everything. And, see if any of them could possibly match our witness description.'

'Sure, I'll get on it now,' Pete said.

Winter gave a frustrated sigh. The stories had checked out so far, but there were those few minutes when the CCTV cameras were off that any one of them could have deposited the head. Equally, he could be barking up the wrong tree and the killer waited until they'd checked the dolmen before he threw it in. He needed to speak to Marek Dubanowski and see what he had to say about that.

He looked at his watch. Winter had arranged to meet Marek, the security guard at the Hougue Bie site in half an hour. He could have asked him to come into the station but he needed to get a feel for visibility at the site, and to look at the CCTV system. With the new knowledge he'd gleaned from the four officers who'd attended, he wanted to see how easy it would have been for somebody to have avoided them and snuck back while they were still on site and before the alarms were reset. The only other option was that it had been one of the five uniformed men themselves who'd used the alarm as an excuse and then flung the head in after the others had searched. That was a real possibility he couldn't ignore.

TWENTY-THREE

La Hougue Bie was still closed to the public and so when Winter arrived, the gate was shut and the place looked deserted.

It didn't take long for Lewis, the site guardian, to appear. When he saw it was Winter, he'd raised his hand and opened the gate.

'Keep having to turn people away,' Lewis said to him as Winter got out of his car.

'You're OK to open up again tomorrow,' Winter replied. 'I presume you've been told?'

'Yes, thank you. That's what we're telling everyone. You here to see Marek? He's in the office.'

Winter stole a glance at the big mound in front of him, the small stone chapel at its crown. For thousands of years it had witnessed people going about their business. Generations after generations. It was quite humbling realising how insignificant one human life was in the context of its history. He wished though that it could speak, not just to share the stories throughout man's history, but to help explain to him how a head could have miraculously arrived deep inside the chamber at its heart, without anybody seeing how it got there.

Marek jumped up from the desk chair when he saw Winter walk into the small office area. They exchanged greetings and Lewis left them to it, heading back out to intercept any other hopeful visitors. Winter noted how tired Marek looked. He was a wiry man, slightly below average height and what Winter's mother would call swarthy looking with a dark beard. It didn't look like he'd always been a night shift security guard.

'Are you back on shift this evening?' he asked him, accepting a mug of something brown and steaming.

Marek nodded. 'I do four nights a week.'

'You find the night shifts hard? I can remember my early career when I had to cover the overnights. Never could get used to having to go to bed so early.'

Marek shrugged. 'My wife works full-time days, we have two children and childcare is expensive so it works for us. I can do the school runs and she takes over so I can come to work.'

'Sorry if you've had to come in earlier today, I hope it hasn't inconvenienced your family,' Winter said, realising that it was still only three o'clock and the schools would be breaking up now.

'It's OK. My wife was able to finish a couple of hours early. She'll make the hours up another time.'

Marek looked a little nervous and Winter realised that the man was probably concerned about his job. He and his wife were typical of so many couples in Jersey who struggled to make ends meet. The island was an expensive place to live, housing costs in particular a big burden. There was a higher percentage of double income earners in each family, just to pay the bills and while incomes were generally higher and taxes lower than the UK, with housing costs taken into account, the island has a larger proportion of its population classed as low income, compared to the UK. It irked Winter that there was always the assumption from outsiders that everyone living here was wealthy and attracted by the more favourable tax regime, when in fact those individuals made up a very small minority of islanders. It was a lovely place to live but it was hard for many families, like Marek's, to survive financially and the gap between the wealthy and the low-income islanders was huge.

'I just wanted to get a better feel for the time frame of when everything happened the other night,' Winter began. 'The alarm went off at just gone eleven p.m.?'

'Yes. I was in here. I walk around the site once every hour, just to check all is OK and I'd been out about half an hour before. I could see the screens, I'd seen nothing.'

'Have you ever had a false alarm before?'

Marek shook his head.

'So what did you do?'

'I went outside straight away. The museum was my first concern and so I checked the doors and windows. Then the honorary police officers arrived. I told them what had happened and they both went off to look around.'

'Which direction did they go in?'

'They checked the museum again and then went around the mound that way.' Marek indicated a clockwise direction with his hand. 'I saw the flashing lights of the States police car coming and so I stayed there ready to speak to them. Then they also went off to check.'

'Did you stay outside while they were looking around?'

'I did until the honoraries came back, then one of them suggested we check the CCTV, see if it caught anything. I was doubtful as I'd been keeping an eye, but I checked anyway.'

'Did they both come with you while you did that?'

'Mmmh.' Marek frowned and thought hard before answering. 'Not all the time, no. Initially they were both there. I'm not a hundred per cent sure how to operate the playback, but one of them had the same system where he worked, and showed me. But it took me a while to look at each camera and they went outside to see if the other officers had found anything and to let them know what we were doing.'

'Together?'

'What do you mean?'

'Did they go outside together?'

Marek looked more stressed. 'I don't know, I was concentrating on the screens. Why?'

'Did you realise that when you looked at the recordings, you stopped the system recording any new images? We have a period of almost twelve minutes when there's no camera output.'

The security guard now looked horrified. 'I didn't know, but we had checked by then. We were all looking; there was nobody here.'

Winter just nodded. 'OK. And after the officers had all left, did you notice anything? Hear anything?'

Marek shook his head vigorously.

Winter asked him a few more questions, but all he was getting back were the same answers as the other four. He thanked Marek and left the office to return outside. From the security office and the car park, you couldn't see the back of the mound where the passage grave entrance was. If everyone had been gathered here, then it was more than feasible for someone to have snuck round and thrown the head in while the cameras were off. He was getting nowhere closer to finding out what had happened, just finding more possibilities.

Winter headed back to the office and slumped into his chair, dejected. He turned on his computer in the hope that somebody had sent him an email with good news, or better still that Saskia had got in touch. He was disappointed on both counts.

'Want to go for a beer?' Jonno appeared at Winter's desk a short while later, eyebrows raised. Winter had been sat staring at his screen, working through the evidence they'd gathered and the statements they'd taken, desperately searching for some kind of lead.

'Not sure I feel up to it, mate,' Winter replied.

'Yup, that's why I'm asking. Haven't missed the long face.'

'Cheers, bud, but I'm OK.'

Jonno sat down next to him and just sat staring at him.

'Really I'm OK.'

Jonno carried on staring at him.

'Look, I think Saskia is in a relationship, that's all,' he whispered to his friend, checking that nobody else in the office could hear him. 'I went round there last night and she had somebody there with her. It was a bit awkward. That and this bloody case because we're getting nowhere.'

Jonno leaned back in the chair and put his hands behind his head.

'You talked to her about it?'

'No.'

Jonno raised his eyebrows and looked at him judgementally.

'I haven't had a chance.'

'You need to, mate. I know what you're like, when it comes to relationships you're a little slow in coming forward.'

'Well thanks for the vote of confidence!'

'Just trying to help.' Jonno smirked, lightening the conversation. 'So you coming for that beer or what?'

'I'll see.'

Winter's mobile started to buzz and vibrate on the desk and *Mum & Dad* came up on the screen.

'I'll leave you to it,' Jonno said and went back to his desk as Winter picked up the call.

'Winter?' It was his mother. 'I'm sorry to call you at work, but can you pop round after work. I really need to talk to you about my friend Enid.'

'Sure,' Winter replied, it would get him off the hook with

Jonno. He appreciated his friend's concern and sometimes talking things through was just what he needed, but not right now. It was too raw.

Winter was just shutting down his computer when his mobile rang again. It was Saskia. He hesitated and then grabbed it and quickly left the office. He wasn't sure what kind of conversation this was going to be, but he'd rather it wasn't in full hearing of his whole team.

'Winter, it's Saskia,' she said needlessly.

'Hi,' he replied, not quite sure what else to say.

'I really need to talk to you, is there any chance you can come round? It's about the case.'

'Yes of course.' Winter's heart had leapt and then dropped again when she said it was about work; but he had to sort his priorities out. 'Shall I bring dinner?'

'No, it's OK as long as you like pizza.'

'I do.'

And that was that. He took a deep breath and got in his car. If he was to continue working with her and they were able to use her valuable skills, then he had to get over his own personal issues. Winter sent a text to his mother saying something had come up with work and he would call her in the morning, then he swallowed his nerves and headed to St Ouen.

TWENTY-FOUR

The more Saskia had thought about Mark Byrne being the killer, the more she became convinced that she could be right. The trouble was, she knew she didn't have a shred of evidence apart from knowing what his personality was like and that he bore a passing resemblance to the photofit. He was in work, always seemed to manage to get himself on the day shifts, and he was due to finish at four thirty p.m. Saskia was ready for him. She'd come up with an excuse to be downstairs near to the exit to the car park, and so while Byrne clocked out from his shift and handed in his keys and security equipment, she had her helmet on and was sitting on her bike, ready to follow him. She knew his address, but she wanted to know if he went straight home after work, and who was at home to greet him.

She was running a big risk that Byrne might spot her behind him, and so she kept well back as she drove, hiding behind other cars so that he didn't spot her motorbike. There were times that some of the country roads were quiet and so she just hung as far back as she could without losing him. When she knew they were getting close to where he lived, she caught up a bit, eager to see what happened when he got home.

Byrne parked his car outside a tired house that clearly needed a bit of maintenance work on its windows and roof. The front garden had been turned over to a parking space. It was semi-detached, with a house next door that would have been identical had it not clearly had some money spent on it in recent years.

Byrne got out and pushed his keys into the front door lock. Saskia had taken her helmet off and pulled her hood over her head to get as close as she could without him seeing. He stepped inside but didn't call out to anyone. The house was in semi-darkness, no lights on. If someone had been home, she'd have expected a couple of lights to be on as the daylight was fading fast.

She watched as a light went on in the front ground floor window and caught a glimpse of an empty room before Byrne walked to the windows and pulled the curtains.

The bedrooms upstairs already had their curtains pulled and so she looked for a way around the back to see if she could spot anything there.

Saskia picked her way down a grassy side strip. The garden was fenced in with old wooden panels that were rotted and broken in places. It gave her a good view of the back of the house. A light was on in the kitchen, but there was nobody in there. It looked as though Byrne had gone upstairs because lights appeared above. Surely if his mother was there, he'd have called out to her, or gone to see her? But then she reminded herself that she was watching a psychopath and he wasn't going to be caring how his mother was feeling or if she was worried because she'd heard a noise.

Saskia looked around the back garden. It was a decent size with a lawn either side of a rough path that led to a garden shed and a wood pile. What was she looking for? What evidence did she expect to find that he was the killer of the two women whose remains they'd found at the dolmen sites?

Saskia was distracted by a small black and white cat which began weaving between her legs, mewing. She crouched down for a few moments and stroked it before movement in the Byrne kitchen caught her eye. Mark had changed and was now standing staring at his open fridge, clearly trying to decide what to have for dinner. Was he cooking for two?

The little black and white cat gave up on Saskia and squeezed between a broken slat in the fence, heading towards a bowl that was placed in the centre of the garden path. It didn't look as though anything was in it, but the cat must have been expecting something because it walked up to it, tail raised, and sniffed. Then it sat down and mewed.

Did Mark or his mother have a cat?

She saw Mark stop what he was doing in the kitchen and look out to the garden; he must have heard the cat, or seen it arrive. Through the kitchen window, a wide shaft of light into the back garden illuminated the cat and the bowl.

Had she totally underestimated Mark? Was he not the cold-hearted monster she thought he was? She'd never have thought he would be the kind of man who'd take care of a cat.

She watched as he bent down to get something and then came to the back door, unlocking it. He must have got some food for the cat. Saskia watched as the door opened and Mark's large bulk filled the entrance.

Only what he had in his hand didn't look like a can of food.

In the time it took Saskia to work out what Byrne was holding, he'd already raised it and fired a bolt at the cat. The little black and white feline didn't stand a chance; it jumped and twisted in the air, barely even able to make a noise, before falling back down onto the lawn. Dead. A crossbow bolt in the front of its chest.

Saskia had to put her hand over her mouth to stop herself from screaming. Her entire body had frozen in shock and she instantly wanted to cry for the poor little cat that Byrne now walked up to, kicked, and then picked up.

He looked up, scanning the fence line, unbalancing Saskia slightly as she instinctively drew back. She could just see him: he'd heard her and now stood watching.

Saskia held her breath. He might still have more bolts for the crossbow and she knew he wouldn't hesitate shooting her with one and then claiming some kind of self-defence later. Or perhaps her body wouldn't be found.

Byrne stood there a few moments longer, listening and watching, then he turned and walked back towards the house. In one hand the cat hung limply by one leg, in the other was the crossbow.

The immediate danger over, Saskia came to her senses and grabbed her mobile from her pocket. She swiped left to get the camera up and quickly took some photographs. He was almost inside and she only just got him as he disappeared from view. She didn't dare to look at the images yet – he might see the light from her phone in the darkness – and so she crept back to her motorbike.

Her legs were shaky and her heart was still racing. She couldn't believe what she'd just witnessed. Somebody's beloved pet had just been executed in cold blood. It was as though he'd set a trap for the purpose. Saskia had no proof that Byrne was the dolmen killer, but she was definitely not going to let him get away with this. She took some deep breaths, trying to calm herself, flashes of childhood traumas screaming in her head as they tried to come to the fore and overwhelm her. Finally, her hand stopped shaking enough for her to be able to turn the ignition on her bike and ride home.

She needed to speak to Winter – and quickly.

TWENTY-FIVE

The second Winter pulled up outside Saskia's cottage, she had the door open. He was reminded of the last time he was there and forced himself to push it out of his mind. This time he walked in through an open doorway, shutting it behind him.

'I've almost finished the profile for you,' Saskia said to him as soon as he was inside, 'but there's something I need to talk to you about first.'

'OK.'

She looked a little unsettled, not nervous or scared, just on edge. Winter wondered if it was because of their last encounter. 'You know you don't need to explain anything to me,' he tried to temper her unease.

Saskia looked at him, confused.

'I mean about the last time I was here,' he continued.

'Oh, yes. I want to talk to you about that too,' she said to him, this time looking him right in the eyes as though trying to search inside his mind. 'But, first we need to catch the dolmen killer.'

Winter didn't get the chance to reply, or feel embarrassed about the fact he'd clearly been obsessing about their last encounter when she hadn't. She'd walked off to the little table and chairs at the back of her sitting room. He followed. On the table was a laptop and two glasses with a bottle of water. She obviously did mean business.

'I'll email you the full profile,' Saskia said to him, settling into one of the chairs and pulling her laptop towards her. 'But the headlines to me are similar to what I've said before. I think the killer has an issue with a female figure in his life. Could be a mother, or could be a partner. He feels as though she controls him and so he takes these women in order to exert some control over them himself. Their ages signify to me that we are most likely looking at a mother figure rather than a wife, and the photofit you sent me would indicate that the man's age is a good twenty to thirty years younger than his victims, so that would back up the mother theory.'

Winter stayed silent, listening and watching her. He could see the passion in her face.

She continued. 'He buries them at the dolmens because of the vestiges of respect he has for her. The dolmens were for elders of the community, and those held in high regard. It's a love-hate relationship he has with this woman, as with so many people who suffer abuse from a loved one. Despite how he feels, he still will crave her love in some way and he can't bring himself to just dump the bodies of his proxy mother. He will likely be living alone, or in a manner which allows him privacy so that he can keep their remains undetected. His mother or partner might, for example, be incapacitated and unable to check on what he's doing. But despite this depraved part of him, he can also be charming and engender trust. Perhaps it's his job and uniform that help with that. He gains the trust of these women and then, when perhaps they start to sense what he's really like, he makes them captive and eventually murders them.'

'So you think that the witnesses were right, that he is a police officer?' Winter asked.

'Not necessarily police, he could be a security guard, fireman, ambulance officer, or a prison officer. Any of these emergency services whereby the uniform instantly encourages trust or there is confusion as to what service he actually works for.'

'Yep, so that's pretty much our working theory at the moment, but is there anything else you can suggest which will help us find out who he is?'

'Geography, we've already covered too. He lives around the area where the victims were taken from and buried.' Saskia hesitated.

Winter waited for her to speak again.

'I've got a potential suspect.'

He was taken aback. 'A suspect? Who? How?'

'It's someone from work.'

'A prison guard?'

Saskia nodded.

'I don't know if he's the dolmen killer,' she said turning her laptop round to show Winter, 'but I saw him shoot a pet cat in cold blood with a crossbow earlier and he looks similar to the photofit and lives in the right area.'

Winter stared at the image on the laptop screen. It was a man in a back garden, holding what he presumed to be a dead cat by one leg and a small crossbow in the other hand. The cat clearly had something sticking from its chest area that looked like a crossbow bolt.

'Why... how did you take this photo? Were you watching him?' he asked Saskia.

She looked slightly embarrassed. 'I was at his house. He apparently lives with his mother still and I wanted to know if he might be the killer.'

'But why would you suspect him?'

'He's a psychopath, a bully. When I saw the photofit image,

and knowing about the witness statements having seen a man in uniform, I just thought it was worth checking out.'

'What's his name?'

'Mark Byrne.'

Winter's mind was racing. 'Did you see anything else, have any other evidence that links him to our dolmen killings?'

Saskia shook her head sadly.

'We found a calendar at Mrs Cunningham's, the second victim's house. On it was written, *M to fix light*. M could be Mark.'

Saskia's eyes suddenly brightened. 'That would fit.'

'We have grounds to get a warrant based on what you witnessed and this photograph. Animal cruelty is wrong whether he's our dolmen killer or not, but I'm going to struggle to persuade my bosses that he could be our killer based on just this and one letter on a calendar.'

Saskia pulled up another photograph, this time of Mark Byrne in his prison uniform.

Winter nodded. 'I can see why he could fit the profile and the photofit, but you said he's a psychopath. What's he doing working at the prison, why isn't he inside it?'

'He gets his kicks from bullying the prisoners, a captive audience, along with the staff. It can be a dangerous environment in prisons and someone like him is able to manipulate situations to his own advantage. I don't know what else he does outside, apart from hurt animals. But, you might also like to know that his dad was murdered when Mark was twenty. Killed in a back alley in St Helier. Nasty piece of work too by all accounts and nobody was ever charged for it.'

'So you're thinking the son, this Mark Byrne, could have done it?'

Saskia shrugged. 'It's possible, obviously I've no knowledge of the case, but knowing what Mark Byrne is like, I wouldn't have put it past him.'

'You know you really shouldn't have gone round to his house,' Winter said to her. 'If he's that dangerous, he could have killed you. You should have called me immediately with your suspicions.'

'I was careful and I left as soon as I saw what he did to the cat. I couldn't tell you before because I had no proof of any wrongdoing.'

Winter was silent again for a few moments, weighing up all he'd just heard. 'One question,' he started, 'you said a couple of days ago to me that you didn't think a psychopath was behind these killings and yet you're telling me that's exactly what Mark Byrne is.'

'I know–' Saskia nodded – 'but well maybe I was wrong.'

'But you've told me that psychopaths are incapable of love and don't care about their victims. That still doesn't fit with your profile and what he does with the bodies.'

Saskia pushed herself back in her chair from where she'd been leaning on the table and furrowed her forehead, looking at Winter.

'I just know that this man is cruel and violent, looks like the witness reported suspect, lives in the same area, and wears a uniform that could be mistaken as a police uniform.'

'Has he ever hurt you?'

Saskia hesitated now. 'He's tried bullying me at work, he's dangerous, sets people against each other, and is physical when he can get away with it. I know why you're asking me this, and yes I guess I am biased against him. But ultimately, it's up to you if you think what I've told you is reason enough to suspect him.'

'It's reason enough to haul him in for animal cruelty, that's for sure,' Winter replied. 'I'll need to get a team together and check this out some more.'

'Thank you.' She smiled at him. 'Would you like that pizza now?'

'You know what,' Winter replied, 'if you don't mind I'll

head back to the station and get the ball rolling on this. If he is our man then we can't waste any time. I'll look at where we're at with his father's killing too.'

Winter reluctantly got up to leave. He could see some of the arguments for suspecting Byrne, but was he their killer? Saskia was in several ways contradicting her own profile of the murderer by suggesting Byrne.

Winter needed to get away and get things straight in his head. The animal cruelty would be an easy way in to paying Mark Byrne a visit and charging him with a crime so that they could interview him and get DNA and fingerprints. If there was a chance that he could end the dolmen killer investigation tonight, then Winter was going to take it.

TWENTY-SIX

Sometimes he felt like she was watching him. Judging him. Wherever he went. Whatever he did.

It was as though her eyes could see inside his head and know all of his most private secrets. Maybe that's why she got so cross with him. Maybe she saw his dirty hidden thoughts.

He'd gone back round later that night and used the spare key to let himself in. She was asleep in bed and so it was easy to gag her and tie her up with no fuss. With the gag around her mouth she couldn't say anything cruel to him. He could remember her kind words and praise, her thanks and her encouragement. He wouldn't let her ruin it.

He'd reassured her, told her that he'd be back to look after her, that she had nothing to worry about. He put the television on and sat her in her chair. The curtains were already pulled, nobody could see them and ruin anything. It was just the two of them. It would be special. He wouldn't feel inadequate, they could be together like a loving mother and son should be.

'I'll come back and watch the television with you.' He'd smiled at her. He put the rug that she sometimes used over her knees and found something else to go around her shoulders. He didn't want her getting cold.

Then he'd left to get some sleep before work. It felt good to know she would be there for him when he'd finished. He just hoped she wouldn't ruin it again and so he wouldn't have to punish her.

He gave her a kiss goodbye and felt the soft warmth of her cheek. The warmth of a loving mother.

TWENTY-SEVEN

Winter left Saskia's and headed straight back to the office. Could she be right? Could this Mark Byrne be their killer? The first thing he did was look him up on the system. As a prison officer, Winter knew he was unlikely to have a criminal record, but there was a chance that there was something in his distant past. If someone had been convicted of crimes as a child, but had a clean record as an adult, then it didn't always preclude them from joining the prison service.

Young Mark Byrne had been pulled over several times and threatened with being taken into care as a child. He was charged with anti-social behaviour and according to his records, had a complex relationship with his parents. The more Winter looked at the man, the more he became a possible suspect for their dolmen killer.

Winter put together the information he had, and his and Saskia's suspicions, and sent it on to Detective Chief Inspector Chris Sharpe. They had enough to go and arrest him for the animal cruelty anyway; what he wanted was the green light for a full search and investigation into Byrne. If he was their killer, Winter wanted to make sure they didn't miss anything.

For once, Sharpe didn't argue with anything that Winter said. Perhaps it was because he knew they had an animal cruelty case against him anyway, or perhaps it was because he was relieved that the suspect wasn't one of their own uniformed staff. Either way, he gave Winter the go ahead to put a team together and go arrest Byrne and search his house.

Things moved quickly then; they decided to go in at five a.m., when they knew Byrne would still be at home. Winter grabbed a couple of hours sleep at the office, and was ready, adrenaline pumping at four thirty a.m. to drive to Byrne's address. As they travelled in convoy along the near empty roads, he hoped and prayed that they were right and could stop the dolmen murderer's killing spree.

Byrne's street was draped with darkness, just a few streetlights standing like showerheads bathing the pavement below them in white light. Winter knew that knocking on the Byrne household's front door was likely to wake up more than just those inside, but they had a job to do. Once everything was in place, he strode up the front path, knocked on the door and rang the bell. There was no immediate response from inside so Winter tried them both again. This time, through the frosted glass in the door, he saw a light come on in the hallway and a large figure heading down the stairs.

There was the metallic clanking of locks being opened and then the door swung open to reveal a big bearded man in a dressing gown, and a face like thunder.

'What's going on?' he said gruffly.

Winter watched as Byrne's face quickly took in the scene in front of him. He had clearly just been woken from a deep sleep but seeing six police officers in your front garden was a quick wake up call.

'Mr Mark Byrne?' Winter said, showing his police badge.

'I'm Detective Inspector Winter Labey and I'm here to arrest you for animal cruelty. My team are going to search your house—'

'Animal cruelty!' Byrne exclaimed. 'I don't have any bloody animals. What are you on about?'

'Step away from the door please, Mr Byrne, so we can go inside and discuss this.'

'No, hang on a minute, you need to explain yourself.'

'I am going to explain myself, Mr Byrne, but unless you'd like the entire neighbourhood to hear our conversation, then I suggest you step back inside your house and let me and my team in. If you don't, then we will arrest you immediately anyway. I have a warrant as you can see.'

Byrne studied him and the paperwork for a moment and then clearly decided that Winter wasn't bluffing. He gave him a look that would have frozen a volcano and then moved further into the hallway.

'Is there anyone else here in the house?' Winter asked.

Byrne shook his head.

'Right, let's go into the sitting room, shall we?' Winter directed him, while the rest of the team piled in and spread out around the house.

'I want to know what you're accusing me of,' Byrne said, rounding on Winter as they walked into the sitting room.

Winter could instantly see the bully in the man. He certainly didn't like to be the one being told what to do, and he used his physical size, even trying to intimidate him.

'You do know I'm a prison officer, right? I'm on the same side as you,' Byrne tried.

'I do, yes. I also know that yesterday evening, you shot a cat with a crossbow.'

'You're kidding me, all this because you think I shot a bloody cat?'

'Sit down please, Mr Byrne.' Winter wanted to reduce his physical bullying stance.

He wasn't about to tell him why they were really there; he first of all wanted to see if the team found anything. He looked around the sitting room, taking in the old-fashioned reclining armchair. Just the sort of armchair that an elderly person might choose. Then his eyes fell on some photographs on the bookshelf.

'I understand this house is registered to a Mrs Christina Byrne, is that your mother?'

Byrne nodded.

'So where is your mother if she's not here now?'

'She went into a care home about six months ago. Costing a bloody fortune, but she needed help.'

'Which care home is that?' Winter asked. He would have to check it out and ensure Byrne wasn't lying.

'Sir,' a voice came from the doorway. 'DS Mark Le Scelleur had a large plastic evidence bag inside which was a crossbow. 'There's a fresh hole in the garden, we're just checking that for the cat,' he added.

Winter turned back to Byrne. 'Do you want to say anything before we find more evidence?'

He shrugged. 'Yeah, I shot a cat. It kept coming into my garden and crapping. I thought there was a right to defend your property. I used it.'

'That cat is no doubt somebody's pet,' Winter replied firmly. 'Why do you have a crossbow?'

'It's not illegal. I shoot rats.'

'Rats.'

'Yup rats. They're always coming around off the fields, so I shoot them.'

'Can I ask you where you were the night before last, Mr Byrne?'

'Here where I usually am. I go to work, make dinner, watch

TV and go to bed. Why? Where am I supposed to have gone? What are you thinking I did? This isn't just about the cat, is it?'

'Can anyone vouch for your whereabouts?'

'No. You might wanna ask the neighbours across the road, the Parkinsons, they like being nosey and seeing what I'm up to.'

Byrne sat on his sofa, his arms defiantly crossed across his chest.

'I'll be back,' Winter said to him. 'DC Everton here will stay with you.'

Winter did a quick walk around the house. It was stuck in a time warp from the 1990s – tired decor, old fashioned ornaments and fading wallpaper. There were three bedrooms upstairs. The main one sported a purple nylon throw on the bed, which looked as though it hadn't been slept in for a while. Byrne's room was at the other end of the corridor. An officer was looking through the drawers and cupboards.

'See if you can find anything that might link him to another property, or a lock-up of some kind,' Winter said to him.

'You'll want to see this, sir,' the officer said. 'The screen was turned off but the computer was left on.' He moved the mouse and the screen instantly lit up with an image of a brutal sex scene where a woman was being degraded by several men. 'There's a lot more and videos too,' the officer added.

'Get that computer taken in and analysed straight away, would you?' Winter said, turning away from the image which repulsed him.

The officer nodded and renewed his searching efforts.

Although the computer might yet yield something that they could charge Byrne with on top of the animal abuse, there was no sign of anything which could link him to the dolmen murders. Winter was beginning to feel the sand starting to shift underneath his feet. Byrne was a very unpleasant individual, but he didn't feel like their man. Nobody was coming to him with evidence they'd found apart from the crossbow. If Byrne was the dolmen killer, surely they'd find something here? Winter headed back downstairs.

'Did you check for a freezer?' Winter asked DS Le Scelleur, who was just coming back into the kitchen from the garden.

'Just this one,' Le Scelleur said, nodding to the one behind Winter. It was a fridge-freezer that was far too small to have fitted in the remains.

'Anything in the shed?'

'Only gardening stuff. No signs of any formaldehyde and no evidence of the victims. On the plus side, we've found the dead cat, and it may not be the only one.'

Winter closed his eyes in frustration. Solving the neighbourhood's disappearing cat situation hadn't been top of his wish list. He wanted to find the man responsible for murdering two innocent women.

The memory of Mrs Byrne's photograph in the sitting room came back to him. Saskia had said it was likely to be a complicated love-hate relationship. Could there be more than just cats buried in the back garden?

An hour later, Winter was forced to take the victory for the cats and charge Byrne with animal cruelty. It was a crime and it was a cowardly thing to do, shooting beloved pet animals, but it wasn't the collar he'd have preferred. They'd called the care home where Mark said his mother was now living and found that he'd told the truth. He hadn't murdered her and buried her in the garden. He was also taken into custody while they investigated the videos and images on Byrne's laptop. From what Winter had seen, it looked as though the women might not be consenting and that would bring other charges if they were found to be illegal. Taking someone like Byrne off the streets was a good success, but cats and extreme pornography weren't Winter's cases. He'd be handing Byrne over to another team.

The dolmen killer was still out there.

TWENTY-EIGHT

FRIDAY

Winter decided to go home for some rest after leaving Mark Byrne's house. Following the adrenaline pump of the dawn raid, he'd crashed. Keeping his eyes open had become a losing battle and if he couldn't get his brain to function, then he was going to be no use to the inquiry. He left his team to process Byrne and look into his movements over the past few weeks, just in case there was another property linked to him where he held the women.

He crawled into his bed at around seven thirty a.m., and slept for three hours. He felt like crap when he woke up, as though he'd been drinking heavily and had a cold coming. He was angry and frustrated that they hadn't found any evidence that Byrne could be their man.

When he looked at his phone, there were fifteen text messages, including one from Saskia and several from his mother.

He'd texted Saskia when they'd finished at Byrne's house, letting her know what they'd found – and not found. Her text was a long apology for having suggested that the dolmen killer could have been Byrne. He replied quickly to say that he didn't blame her. Anyone would have put two and two together with what they knew of the man and see that it was a possibility. The photofit, living at home still, his general character, and where he lived. All potential clues that he could have been their suspect. But he wasn't. It was a set of coincidences. At least there would be a family whose missing pet could be explained, although last he'd heard, it looked as though there were two other cat skeletons, along with some seagulls buried in his back garden.

Winter reassured Saskia and then read his mother's texts. She'd also called several times while he'd been asleep as he had four missed calls from her.

> Please call me as soon as you get this. I'm very worried about Enid.

Her next one was even more direct.

> Call me urgently.

Winter tried her mobile, but it rang out, so he dialled home. His father answered.

'Is Mum there? She's been trying to get hold of me.'

'No. She decided you were too busy and has gone round to Enid's house herself. She's been very worried about her. They were supposed to meet up for coffee yesterday and she didn't show, plus she's not answering her phone. Your mum knows where she hides the spare key and so she's going to check on her.'

'Bloody hell, why didn't you go with her, Dad?'

'I was still in my pyjamas, she wouldn't wait for me. Just drove off. You know what your mother's like when she gets a bee in her bonnet.'

'Right, what's the address?'

'9 Le Grand Clos de Catillon,' his father said, clearly reading something.

'That's not far from Hougue Bie,' Winter thought aloud.

'That's right, I'm never quite sure if it's St Saviour or Grouville.'

'Dad, is Enid still living on her own?'

'Yes, you know her Bill died a while back now, never looked after himself that man...'

'I've got to go, Dad, sorry.' Winter ended the call. A woman in her seventies living on her own and no one had heard from her. It could be the tiredness making him paranoid, or perhaps his desperation to find the killer, but there was a burning sensation in his stomach which told of the fear which now stalked through his mind.

He slammed into the bathroom, splashing some cold water on his face, and headed straight out the door, not bothering to change from last night's clothes. Whatever had happened, his mother might need his help, and if his worst fears were realised, she might also be in danger.

TWENTY-NINE

Saskia had been on tenterhooks after Winter had left her cottage. As soon as she'd told him that she suspected Mark Byrne, she had started to doubt herself. Winter was right, she didn't think that the dolmen killer was a psychopath, so how could Mark Byrne be the killer? And yet there was the description of the man the neighbours had seen and the sheer cold-blooded cruelty she'd witnessed with the cat. The latter certainly backed up her psychopathic diagnosis. She was glad that she'd managed to get that photograph and that he was going to have to answer for what he'd done to the poor creature. The downside was that this was probably the final nail in the trust coffin for Winter. He'd never believe her again if Byrne had nothing to do with the murders.

When the text came through from Winter the next morning to say they'd found nothing to link Byrne to the dolmen killings, she was already awake. Her mind had run through the scenarios a thousand times and she'd resigned herself to thinking that perhaps Winter losing his trust in her was a good thing. If he never wanted to see her again or trust her profiling then it would make things easier for her. Being around him had been difficult at times because she'd wanted so much more. This way, she would have less reason not to move on again. Leave Jersey.

Later that morning she was going to break a trust that she'd protected and suffered for all her life: her brother's. He was the reason she'd come back to the island and now she had an appointment with Jackie Slater where she was about to expose not only him, but also herself. She had no way of knowing how Jackie would react to what she was going to tell her. Would she think that Saskia was the psychopath coming to destroy their relationship? Would she even believe that they were siblings? There were so many ways their conversation could go and a lot of them weren't good.

Saskia had barely anything from her childhood; most mementos had brought back bad memories and were long since thrown away, and things that she'd liked had been lost in the fire that David started when he was almost ten years old. After that they'd moved so often, and Saskia could usually only take whatever fitted into a rucksack with her.

The one thing she did have to prove her connection with him was a photograph of her and David together when he was about seven and she was nearly nine. It had been taken at a school event which was how she'd managed to get a photographic record of them. They never took any images as a family. Had never even had a camera as far as she could remember, and there was certainly no money for mobile phones as kids. She kept the photograph in her bedside table drawer, away from any prying eyes but where she knew she had it close. Once she was ready to go and see Jackie, Saskia had gone to the drawer and taken it out. She'd spent a moment looking at the two young faces in the image, trying to remember the girl who looked back at her. So much had happened since that day. In some ways she was proud of what that girl had achieved since then, but in other ways, she was still stuck there, standing awkwardly, looking at her brother who was staring at the camera as though he was the only subject of the photograph. The only person in the room. He'd always made her feel that way. Saskia tucked the worn image into a small notebook and put it in her bag as she set off to go and meet her brother's girlfriend and shatter his perfect image. On the way, she stopped off to pick up something else too. Some more proof, just in case it was needed.

The venue for their meeting was a hotel café in town. Jackie had suggested the Hotel de France as it was easy for parking and on the opposite side of St Helier to David's office, so as to ensure there was no risk of him seeing them. The café also had indoor and outdoor tables and it wasn't noisy, so easy to talk.

When Saskia arrived, Jackie was already there sitting at a sofa table, looking every part the switched-on businesswoman that she was. Had Saskia misjudged her brother? Was Jackie fine and he wasn't a threat to her after all? Saskia was so nervous. She'd already nearly turned round several times on the drive over and she was slightly late because she'd had to go to the toilet beforehand and give herself a talking to in the mirror. What she was about to do, there would be no going back from. Once David found out that she'd betrayed him – and he was bound to know it was her – he would no longer tolerate her as his sister. Any selfish loyalty he felt towards her because she helped him to live successfully in society would be obliterated. And yet she couldn't stand by and let him hurt people. Saskia walked forward to greet Jackie. She had to do this.

'Hi, Jackie.'

'Alice Moody?' Jackie asked smiling, using the pseudonym that Saskia had used to book their meeting.

Saskia hesitated, sitting down opposite Jackie.

'That's the name I used on the phone, yes, but actually my birth name is Saskia Carter. I'm David's sister.'

'Oh!' Was all Jackie said at first, the surprise registering on her face. 'I didn't know David had a sister? Does he know you're here?'

'No he doesn't, and it's him I want to talk to you about.' Saskia paused again, taking a big breath and looking at the woman in front of her. Jackie's face had switched from warm greeting to wary defensiveness. But there was no point in delaying what she had to say, so she just got on with it. 'I know this is all going to be a bit of a shock, but I've asked to see you today because I'm concerned that your life may be in danger.'

'What the hell? Is this some kind of a joke?' Jackie switched mode again, looking decidedly suspicious and reaching for her mobile phone which she'd placed on the table in front of them. 'Why don't I call David?'

'No.' Saskia's hand shot out and hovered above Jackie's which was inches from her phone. 'Please don't call David yet. All I ask is five minutes of your time to listen to me and then it's up to you what you do.'

Jackie stared at her face, eyes narrowed, studying her. 'I've no idea who the hell you are,' she replied, looking around nervously to ensure there wasn't anybody else about to be sprung on her.

'I'm the prison psychologist at La Moye. You can look me up. I use our mother's maiden name nowadays, Monet, and the reason I do that is because I wanted to distance myself from our father. He is a convicted serial killer, and he's in prison in the UK. You can look him up too. Edward Carter. He was known as the Nightingale Strangler and is currently serving a life sentence in Durham prison. But the critical point is that he's a psychopath, and so is my brother, David.'

Saskia stopped for a moment, taking a breath. Her mouth felt dry like sandpaper and she could feel that her blood pressure had risen, giving her a tight feeling in her head. Jackie was now a picture of incredulity; her mouth had opened as she listened, and her face grown paler. Gone was the flush of anger.

'So you're saying that David is a psychopath?' she reiterated.

'Yes.'

'David and I have been meeting every week,' Saskia continued. 'It was something I told him he had to do in order for him to be able to manage his psychopathy. There's no treatment but by constantly reminding him what he has to lose if he doesn't live by society's rules, I've managed to keep him from doing anything that could get him into trouble. Psychopaths are risk takers, they don't fear consequence, they think only of themselves and they are incapable of loving another human being.'

Jackie had slumped back into the sofa, her taught defiant body language deflated.

'So you're saying he doesn't care about me at all?'

'Not in the way that you or I would care for someone.' Saskia tried not to be too harsh. 'Psychopaths can be superficially charming and attentive, but it's all a surface effect.'

'Why are you telling me all this now? Why if you've been meeting with him all this time?' Jackie asked frowning.

'Because he says that he doesn't need our meetings anymore, which is a huge warning sign to me that he's slipping into doing what he wants without regard for others. Because he told me that you are very tired, getting forgetful, getting dementia like your mother, and that you are considering putting him as a co-signatory on the house and business. I don't think that's a coincidence.'

'Oh my God, yes, ever since Allan's murder I've just not been on top form. I've had to cancel loads of evenings out with my friends because I've just been too tired. Brain fog. I thought it was the menopause or the stress of Allan's death.'

'I suspect he's drugging you somehow and he's starting to isolate you from those who will notice anything untoward.'

'Allan!' Jackie suddenly exclaimed. 'David hated Allan and he was killed the first weekend I went away without David.'

Saskia took a big breath. 'I don't know if David had anything to do with Allan's murder. I'm hoping not because the police have charged his boyfriend, but I do know that David somehow came across your necklace and took it.'

'No, this is all crazy.' Jackie sat back up again, energised. 'David wouldn't do that to me. You're describing a completely different man. How do I know any of this is true? I don't know you.'

'This is a photograph of David and I when we were children. If you google the Nightingale Strangler, you'll find plenty online about our father, Edward Carter. And this is the necklace that David asked me to look after.' Saskia took out a small tin which she'd just dug up from its hiding place. 'He told me it was for your birthday, that he'd bought it. That was before Allan was killed, before you went away. It wasn't until I found out that your necklace had been stolen and never recovered, that I realised it must be this one.' She opened the tin and took out the gemstone, showing it to her discreetly.

Jackie gasped and looked as if she might burst into tears.

'I know this is a lot to take in. I'm sorry, but I had to tell you. I'm worried that he's slipping into a place where he thinks he can do anything he wants and not have to face any consequences.'

'Are you saying that you're telling me this so he doesn't end up in prison?' Jackie's eyes narrowed and she scanned Saskia's face.

'No, I'm telling you this because I don't want something bad happening to you and it ending up on my conscience. I have tried to keep my brother safe throughout our lives, to help him live a good life, but I can't control him and I can't just stand by and let him turn into our father.'

Jackie slumped back onto the seat again. 'I need something bloody stronger than coffee,' she said to her.

To Saskia it looked as though she'd aged five years in just five minutes.

'He's been so attentive lately. Always pouring me drinks

and taking care of me. I've been convinced that I'm losing it, writing the wrong appointment times in my phone calendar, stuff like that.' She looked down at her phone, then suddenly back up at Saskia. 'He has my password. I told him ages ago. So he could be going into my phone and editing stuff. Shit!'

It was one of, if not the most, stressful conversations of Saskia's life. Jackie questioned her some more about David and tested her to ensure she was his sibling.

'I just can't believe that I've been sleeping with a psychopath.' Jackie shook her head.

'I know it's hard to take in,' Saskia said to her quietly.

'The thing is, I can believe you,' Jackie said to her. 'Two months ago I wouldn't have, but lately there have been too many things which made me suspicious and knowing this makes it all fall into place. You know I stupidly thought he did genuinely love me. Some of my friends said he was just a gold digger, but others believed in him too. He was so attentive and charming. But lately it's gone up a gear or two. He can't do enough for me and I've been so tired. He's been the one suggesting I don't overdo things and cancel on my friends. And he's been pressurising me about putting his name on the house and business. If he really loved me, he wouldn't care about that would he?'

Jackie looked at Saskia, her eyes filled with tears. Then her face hardened and she swiped at her eyes with the back of her hand. Saskia saw the businesswoman return.

'So where do we go from here?' Jackie asked.

'That's down to you.'

'Well, obviously I want to involve the police,' Jackie replied.

'He's not done anything illegal yet – that we know.'

'Drugging me, gaslighting me...' Jackie said to her.

'There's no proof of that yet and it's hard to prosecute. It would be his word against yours at the moment.'

'You've got my necklace.'

'The necklace doesn't prove that David stole it, all it does is prove that I have it – that's going to hurt me more than it will hurt him.'

'Well, I want it back,' Jackie said, holding out her hand.

'I'm sorry but I understand that you've been paid by the insurance for the loss so I'm going to have to lose this.'

'You can't, it's mine,' Jackie said.

'Please, Jackie. I have put my career and my freedom on the line to come here and warn you. I cannot be dragged into this in any way. None of this is my fault. I became a psychologist because I thought I would be able to find a way to cure my brother. I've spent my life protecting him and guiding him, monitoring his psychopathy to ensure he's not a threat to himself or anyone else. This has been a massive decision for me to come here and talk to you like this. I'm betraying his trust. But, for whatever reason, I think he's crossed the line and I can't now say that he's not going to hurt you. I don't want that. If I can somehow encourage David to realise what route he's heading down, then maybe I can prevent him from ending up in prison. There are plenty of psychopaths who live in society and don't harm people, at least not physically. They manipulate with their charm, but it's all for their own gain. It's your choice what you do now, whether you stay with David or ask him to leave.'

'Well, I'm hardly going to let him stay, am I? I'd be constantly worrying he's about to murder me. I couldn't ever trust him. Should I tell him that I've spoken to you?' Jackie asked tentatively.

'I would ask you not to please. He doesn't have any family loyalties or love. It might not end well for me.'

Jackie studied her for a few moments again, taking in what she'd just said.

'Can I speak to you again if I need advice?'

'Yes of course, you have my number as Alice Moody.'

. . .

Saskia talked with Jackie for an hour, but it was the longest hour of her life. By the time she'd finished, she was exhausted and just sat in her car, her eyes closed thinking about what she'd just done. Not only did she feel like the world's worst betrayer, but she also felt like the world's biggest failure. She'd spent her whole life trying to ensure David never ended up labelled as a dangerous psychopath and now she'd just told someone that was exactly what he was. All the personal sacrifices she'd made had been for nothing.

She felt drained, but she also knew it had been the right thing to do. She knew in her heart that Jackie was in danger and that David's psychopathy had become too strong for Saskia to control. In the prison environment, she could manage the psychopaths she looked after with strict boundaries and rules. Out here, David was free to do what he wanted and that had clearly become too tempting for him. Saskia's life and relationships were unravelling fast. First Winter and now David. Perhaps it really was time to move on again.

THIRTY

Winter arrived at Enid Baxter's house on blue lights. He would never forgive himself if something had happened to his mother. She'd tried to call him and ask for his help and he'd just ignored her. As he came to a halt at the address his father had given him, he spotted his parents' car parked up out front. There was no sign of his mother and the curtains in the property were drawn closed.

Winter jumped out the car and ran up the path, knocking loudly on the front door. He waited. There was no reply. He knocked again.

'Enid, Mrs Baxter?' he shouted. 'It's Winter Labey, can you open the door?'

He stepped back, scanning the house windows for any signs of life. Nothing.

Winter took out his mobile and called his mother's number. It rang but she didn't pick it up. Then he heard it, the daft ringtone that she had which told her it was her son calling. It rang off. Winter dialled again. There it was ringing out, he bent down and pushed the letter box, and the sound became louder. It was coming from inside.

'Mum!' he called out.

Winter was beginning to feel desperate now. Something was definitely up. They'd have heard him knocking – and why wasn't his mother answering her phone? If they'd gone out for a walk, she would have taken it with her.

He was tired, paranoid and extremely worried about his mother. Winter ran around the perimeter of the property, looking for another way into the house. He scaled a wall to get into the back garden. Still no signs of life. He peered in through the kitchen window and felt his stomach lurch into his throat. There were some empty and full cans of soup sat on the side.

'Mrs Baxter? Mum?' He banged on the window.

Nothing.

He tried the back door to find it was locked. There was nothing else to do. Winter took a step back and brought his elbow up and smashed the glass pane. There was no time to waste: his mother and her friend could be in danger.

Winter paused and listened once he'd opened the back door, his police training ensuring that he didn't run blindly into a dangerous situation. But there was nothing. No sound at all. As he walked through the kitchen, he got on his mobile and called Jonno.

'Jonno, I've just forced entry into number 9 Le Grand Clos de Catillon, I might need assistance as I have reason to be concerned for the homeowner, Mrs Enid Baxter. Stay on the line with me, would you?'

Winter didn't wait for a reply and walked forward cautiously.

'Mrs Baxter?' As he reached the hallway he could see the sitting room door was open. There was a handbag lying on the floor as though it had been thrown. Its contents had spilled out, including a mobile phone. It was his mother's.

'Jonno, I need backup,' Winter said to his friend, rushing

into the sitting room. He could barely get the words out, he was so breathless with fear. The vision of the beheaded victims he'd seen in the past week flashing through his mind. His heart was racing so fast that it became one continuous crescendo of beats. What was he going to find?

As he turned away from the handbag and looked around the room, there in front of him, sitting tied to an armchair was an elderly woman. Her eyes closed, mouth open, skin almost blue it was so pale. 'We need an ambulance!' Winter shouted to his phone and then put it in his pocket.

'Enid? It's Winter Labey. Can you hear me?' he said to her as he crossed to see if he could help. He untied the gag from her mouth and felt for a pulse. It was there but weak.

He scanned the room quickly, nothing else to see here. Where was his mother?

Winter ran up the stairs, checking the bedrooms and the bathroom. There was no sign of his mother and there was no sign of anyone else. He called his father.

'Dad, has Mum come home?'

'No. I thought you were going to Enid's to speak to her there?'

'I'm here, Dad, there's no sign of her. If she turns up, call me immediately.'

'What do you mean no sign of her? Has she had an accident on the way?'

Winter paused a moment, knowing that what he said next could panic his father. He could already hear the concern in his voice.

'No. Her car's here.'

'Well, have you called her mobile?' his dad replied sharply.

'Dad, her mobile and handbag are here too,' Winter said gently.

'What about Enid, does she know anything?'

'She's unconscious. I'll see if the ambulance crew can bring her round.'

Winter heard his dad mumble something. He didn't quite hear the words, and he didn't need to. He knew it was the realisation that something bad might have happened to his wife.

'Dad, Dad, are you OK?'

There was a strangled throat clearing sound and then his father's voice came to his ear, weak and broken. It had aged two decades in the two minutes they'd been talking. 'I'm fine. Find her, Winter.'

'I will, Dad. I'll find her, I promise.'

Jonno and DC Sarah Fuller, were first to arrive at the house, pulling up outside at around the same time as the ambulance. Winter heard their sirens and let them all in.

'It's him, the dolmen killer,' he said to Jonno as his friend rushed up the path towards him. 'I think he's taken my mother.'

'Your mother? What's she doing here?'

'It's her friend, Enid's house.' Winter paused to tell the paramedic where to go. 'She's in there, right-hand side. Possibly held without food and drink for a couple of days.' Winter looked back to Jonno. 'Where's he taken her?'

'And you've searched the whole house? She's definitely not hiding anywhere?'

He shook his head.

'Maybe she didn't actually go inside?' Jonno offered, trying to stop his friend from panicking further. 'Maybe she's gone on an errand or something.'

'Her handbag has been thrown on the floor. She went inside. There was a spare key. She must have disturbed him.'

Winter was starting to feel light-headed and paused a moment to lean on the nearest car.

'Let's get you out of here.' Jonno took charge. 'Sarah, you secure the scene and get forensics in ASAP.'

'It's my fault,' Winter said to his friend. 'She was trying to get me to help and I was too busy working. I should have listened.'

'It's not your fault, mate. The only person to blame here is whoever is doing this to these women.'

Winter nodded but he didn't really agree. This was his fault and now his mother could be dead, but he allowed Jonno to lead him away from the house and to his car.

'My mum's car is still here,' Winter remembered, and pointed to her red Ford Focus. 'He must have taken her in his car. We need to see if anyone saw anything, or if there's any CCTV.' Winter started to click back into work mode and scan the houses around them.

'We will, mate, but you're going to need to sit this one out. You've had a big shock and you're personally involved now.'

'No. No way, I need to find my mother.' Winter pulled his arm out of Jonno's grip and stepped away from him, horrified.

'You know that as soon as the Beak hears this, he'll pull you off the case. You'd make that decision too if it was one of us.'

Winter stared at his friend for a few moments and then looked away. He knew Jonno was right. Detective Chief Inspector Sharpe, or the Beak as they called him, wasn't going to allow him to carry on when there was a clear conflict of interest because his own mother had been taken by the dolmen killer he was investigating. He had to think and act fast.

The ambulance crew came out the house carrying a stretcher with Enid on it, still unconscious.

'Is she going to be alright?' Winter asked them.

'We hope so. Looks like she was dehydrated and has a little hypothermia. With fluids she should pick up quite quickly.'

'We need her to tell us who did this,' Winter said to them. 'He's taken another woman. Her life could be in danger.'

'She's still unconscious, but maybe in a couple of hours she'll come round,' the paramedic replied hopefully.

Winter wasn't sure they had a couple of hours. The dolmen killer could be hurting his mother right now.

THIRTY-ONE

Back at police HQ, the office was in overdrive. Winter knew from the sympathetic glances that everyone was putting an extra ounce into their work because it was now personal. He'd just logged into his computer when the Beak marched in.

'Winter, can I have a word in my office please?' he said to him. The tone wasn't harsh for once, and he even said please, but Winter knew what was coming.

'I'm so sorry to hear your mother is missing,' he started. 'You know you don't have to be here. Go home and take care of yourself and your father.'

'I do have to be here. I have to find her. I can't sit at home just worrying, I need to do my job.'

'Winter, you realise I'm going to have to ask you to step aside from leading this investigation, you're too personally involved now.'

Winter couldn't bring himself to agree, even though he knew it was the right decision.

'I'm going to take over the investigation. We all want to find your mother and ensure no harm comes to her, DI Labey. I'm calling an urgent team meeting now to review what we have.'

'But I can still contribute, right? I've been across all that we've gathered so far, it makes sense.'

Sharpe narrowed his eyes and thought for a few moments.

'I get how you're feeling. I would be the same...' He paused, as though wrestling with himself. 'Look, as long as you understand that I'm in charge and you are to remain on the periphery of the investigation, then your input will be welcomed, but I'll make the operational decisions. Is that clear?'

'Yes, sir,' Winter replied. It was the best he was going to get and he knew that Sharpe could have just insisted he went home, but there was no way he could walk out the office and sit at home worrying while his colleagues got on with the job. He had to help find his mother.

'Let us have anything you know about Mrs Baxter. I'm afraid she's still unconscious but the hospital is going to call the second she wakes up.'

The briefing room was full and so were the volume levels. Everyone was talking about the case and the urgency to help DI Labey find his mother. It was personal for them all now. When Sharpe walked to the front of the room, they instantly fell silent.

'I don't need to stress the urgency,' he said to them, throwing a quick glance in DI Labey's direction.

Winter had positioned himself at the back, using the physical distance to make it look as though he wasn't a part of the investigation, let alone in charge anymore.

'The search at Mark Byrne's house has not yielded any evidence apart from the animal cruelty and a potential charge relating to downloading and viewing extreme pornography. He also has a solid alibi because we were there with him at the time Mrs Labey went missing,' Sharpe said to the room. 'We know that Mrs Labey went round to her friend, Enid Baxter's house, at just gone nine a.m. this morning because she was concerned that she hadn't heard from her. She knew where Mrs Baxter kept the spare key to her house and so would have let herself into the property. That key is now missing. We know all this because she told her husband what she was going to do. A search is still underway at Mrs Baxter's home, but so far it's the same set-up as we found at the other two victims' homes, but thankfully Mrs Baxter is still alive. Have any of the fingerprints taken from the first two victims' homes matched up?'

'We have one possibility, sir,' Trudy Hayman, a crime scene manager, spoke now. 'Most surfaces had been wiped, so this again fits with the theory that the killer is somehow connected to the police or security services, because he's forensically aware. However, we have a couple of partials from Sandra Cunningham's house that match with a clear set found at Barbara Smith's.'

'And I take it no matches on the database?'

'I'm afraid not, sir.'

'So come on, what do we have? There must be a lead.'

'Sir.' DC Edwards stood up. 'We still have the five who were on site at the time that the head was found at Hougue Bie. It's still quite feasible that one of them used the excuse of being at the site to attend the alarm, in order to deposit the head. All five are either police officers, honoraries, or a security guard, so all five could fit the witness description of a man in uniform.'

'But if the fingerprints found at the victims' homes are correct, then that would discount our two States police officers because theirs would be on the database.'

'Yes, sir.'

'Let's go through and prioritise the La Hougue Bie five. Have we cross-referenced them to the profile that Saskia Monet has delivered?'

'Not yet, sir, we can do that now.'

'Get on it then, that should have been done.'

'What else do we know about our killer?'

'It's possible that his name may begin with an M as the second victim had a calendar entry for a light to be fixed by "M",' DC Edward replied.

'What's our potential suspects' names then?'

'Alec Jeune, Michael Rault, and Marek Dubanowski, plus our two PCs, Matthew Drew and Scott Askew.'

'Do any of them have beards?' Sharpe asked.

'PC Matthew Drew does, sir,' DC Edward said, almost apologetically to the room, well aware that any suspicion on one of their own was uncomfortable. 'DI Labey, you interviewed Alec Jeune, Michael Rault and Marek?'

All eyes swivelled to the back of the room where Winter had been sitting on a table.

'None of them had beards,' he replied.

'Beards can be grown and shaved off, so we can't rely on that, and we've got no confirmation that the fingerprints at the two scenes are definitely linked, so I want all five of the Hougue Bie suspects contacted. Where were they this morning? Do they have concrete alibis? Do they fit the profile we have of our killer? And I want a team checking every single camera we can find into and out of the area where Enid Baxter lives. Cross-reference the number plates with those of our five possibles.'

Sharpe stopped and looked at the faces staring back at him.

'I want someone down at the hospital too. The second that Mrs Baxter comes round we need to be asking her who did this to her.' He hesitated and threw an awkward glance towards Winter. 'And I want an officer stationed at every dolmen in the island. Get to it.'

The meeting broke up and everyone scarpered to their various workstations, or out the building to make enquiries. Winter went and sat back down at his desk, shoulders sagging and head hanging. This was his fault. He'd been distracted, too wrapped up in his own personal angst to concentrate on finding the dolmen killer, or to answer his mother's phone calls. Now his mother might be the next victim. The thought of her being decapitated and ending up on Dr Chaudhry's examination table made him feel sick.

'Why don't you go home and sit with your dad for a bit,' Jonno said to him, appearing at his desk with a cup of tea.'

Winter shook his head. 'Thanks. No, his friend is with him. If I was there I'd just wind him up more because I wouldn't be able to sit still. At least here I might be able to help.'

'Sir,' DC Edwards came up to him, 'you said that Michael Rault didn't have a beard when you spoke to him, didn't you?'

Winter looked at the young detective's face, he seemed flush with excitement.

'Yes. He was clean shaven.'

'Well, this is a recent photograph of Michael Rault at a parish event.' DC Edwards turned his laptop round to show Winter an image of a group of parish officials and honorary police officers, one of whom was Rault, who was sporting a thick black beard.

Winter's heart leapt.

'Get on to Alec Jeune and ask him if he knows when Michael shaved his beard off.'

'Let me pull up what we know about him,' Jonno said, logging into the computer next to Winter.

'News?' Sharpe had walked over, alerted by the sudden flurry of activity.

'One of the honorary officers had a beard, just like the one that our photofit suspect had.'

'Name also begins with M,' Jonno added. 'Michael Rault.'

'But didn't you say that they were all clean shaven when you spoke to them?'

'Yes. He was. We're just trying to find out when he might have shaved it off.'

At that moment, DC Edwards came tearing back towards them, making all three men look up. 'He had his beard when they were at La Hougue Bie. Alec Jeune is definite about that.'

Edwards looked from one face to another, his eyes expectant.

'So why shave that morning?' Sharpe asked aloud.

'Because the photofit was out in the media that morning and had been circulated to all the honoraries the day before. He must have seen it and shaved his beard off straight away before he came in to see Winter,' Jonno said. 'And he fits the profile too. Still lives at home with his mother. That's what Saskia highlighted. He also works at a DIY store in town. Didn't we think that maybe the killer was doing some odd jobs to help these women initially?'

'Yes. That totally fits with the M who fixed Sandra Cunningham's light,' DC Edward agreed.

Winter was listening and watching his friends and colleagues, but his head was spinning so fast that he felt as though he was sitting in a fog squinting to see them, their voices muffled. Had he sat opposite the man who had brutally murdered those two women and now held his mother captive? The quietly spoken man who in Winter's post-lunch slump had lulled him into believing he couldn't be a suspect? He'd been tired and distracted that day, not on top form. He hadn't pushed the interview hard enough.

'Have we managed to get hold of this Michael Rault and find out if he has an alibi?' Sharpe asked.

'Not yet, sir, no. He isn't answering his mobile.'

'Ring the shop, see if he's gone into work, and call the mother.'

Winter couldn't sit down at his desk any longer. While his team made phone calls to track down Michael Rault, he paced back and forth, trying to listen in to the various phone calls. All the while, his head was filled with images of his mother trying to defend herself from attack, her voice calling out to him for help. He felt useless just hanging around in the office; he should be out there right now searching for her. But where?

'OK, quick update.' Sharpe's voice cut through the office noise and the traumatic videos on loop in his head. 'Michael Rault hasn't been into work for two days. The last time he was there, he had a beard. His mother claims that he went into work this morning as usual. And the shop manager also confirmed that Michael often bought various items in the DIY store to help elderly people with odd jobs. I think we have a strong suspect. I want a team pulled together, we need to go and interview the mother and see if she knows where her son could have gone. And get his car licence plate out there, see if we can track his car.'

Winter travelled with Jonno in his car to the Rault house, which was right in the centre of Saskia's geographical profile map. Her face came to him on the drive, as though somehow trying to reassure him that they were onto the right man and his mother was going to be OK. He and Jonno had travelled in near silence, both of them knowing that the other was considering the unspoken fear of what they might find when they reached the address.

On the way, Winter had called his father to let him know that they had a suspect. 'It's just going to be a matter of time now, Dad, we're onto him. Mum will be home soon.'

His father had barely spoken. Winter could hear the pain in his voice, cracked and brittle with it. When he'd ended the phone call, it had been with a heavy heart.

Winter knew he wouldn't be able to go into the house with the rest of the team – and in all honesty, he didn't want to. He had no idea what they were going to find in there and even the thought of what could have befallen his mother made him want to run and hide. He had the urge to put his hands over his ears and squeeze his eyes tight shut, as though he could somehow block all this out and pretend it wasn't happening. But he couldn't, and instead he'd taken some comfort from childhood memories of times when he'd been scared or hurt himself. The loving hugs that his mother had given him, the knowledge when he looked in her eyes that she loved him.

So why couldn't he have stopped working for just half an hour to help her out! What kind of a son had he proven to be? One thing he knew for sure, was that if she was in the Rault house alive, he wanted to be there to comfort her, and to watch the man who'd murdered two women and kidnapped his own mother put into handcuffs and locked away.

Winter waited in the car outside the property as the team prepared to go in. Every second that ticked by seemed like an hour. He had to fight the urge to just get out of the car and run into the house, looking for her. As it was, he had to grasp hold of his knees to stop them fidgeting and to provide some kind of solid grounding that would keep him in the car.

He watched as some officers went round the back of the house, ready to stop anyone from trying to escape, and once everyone was in place, the team had hammered loudly on the front door.

Nobody answered. They gave another verbal warning, and when that too went unanswered, the battering ram was brought forward and used to smash through the wooden door. It was all over quickly. He heard the shouts of 'clear' as officers went from room to room. After fifteen minutes, Jonno came back out to talk to him.

'She's not here, mate, and there's no sign that she's been here either.'

Winter let go of the breath he'd been holding.

'No sign of Rault either,' Jonno continued. 'We know his car's gone so we are combing the island right now to try and trace it. His mother's in there, limited mobility which was why she didn't answer the door.' His friend paused a moment, sympathy written across his face. 'It's him, mate. There's a garden shed. Took us a few minutes to get inside and when we did it was like a scene from a horror movie. A whole load of badly stuffed animals staring at you, an old chest freezer, and two chairs. One of the armchairs has a spike coming out of it, and there are bottles of formaldehyde. I'm going to bet that spike is where he put their heads.'

'Did you check the freezer?' Winter's voice sounded like a stranger's to his own ears.

'Yeah. Empty except for a dead magpie.'

Winter quite honestly didn't know whether to smile or cry. He was so relieved to hear that his mother hadn't been doused in formaldehyde, or shoved into a chest freezer, but on the other hand they were no closer to finding her and that meant she was still in danger.

'Doesn't his mother know where he is?'

Jonno shook his head. 'She thought he was at work. Just keeps saying that none of this surprises her and he's a complete waste of space. He fits Saskia's profile to a tee, mate.'

Winter's stomach twisted and the pounding that had started in his head earlier grew worse.

'Where is he, Jonno? Where would he have taken my mother?'

THIRTY-TWO

Saskia called into work sick after her meeting with Jackie. She really wasn't up to speaking or seeing anyone. She felt incredibly vulnerable and she knew that when she felt like this, she could easily make a mistake when interviewing a prisoner, which would have consequences for her and the interviewee.

She'd gone home and lain on the sofa, where she was quickly joined by Bilbo. At first her head had been swimming with various scenarios of David finding out that it was her who warned Jackie off him. Most of them were violent scenes; occasionally she tried to fool herself that it would all be absolutely fine and he'd be grateful that she'd stepped in and prevented him from doing something he might regret. If only he had the capability of regret!

At some point she and Bilbo both fell asleep, the emotional stress having wrung her out.

Saskia obviously needed the sleep because it was only her mobile phone ringing which woke her. She looked at the time: she'd been out for at least an hour and a half. She didn't recognise the number that was calling and so assumed it must be something for work.

'Hello, Saskia Monet,' she said.

'Saskia, it's Jonno. We need your help urgently.'

'Jonno!' she said in surprise. She could hear the tension in his usually chilled-out voice. 'What's happened?'

'Winter's mother has been taken by the dolmen killer. We know who he is now: it's a guy called Michael Rault, an honorary officer. That's how he gained their trust, and he works in a DIY store so he did some odd jobs, helping people with making sure their homes were secure, which was how he chose his victims. I'm at his house now; he lives here with his mother who thinks he's little more than what's on the bottom of her shoe by the sounds of it.'

Saskia didn't reply straight away – she was totally floored by Jonno's first statement, let alone the stream of information that followed.

'He's taken Winter's mother?'

'Yes. She was visiting a friend – she'd been concerned about her and turned out to be rightly so as she was nearly his third victim. She's in hospital, but Mrs Labey is nowhere to be found and neither is the killer.'

'Winter must be beside himself.'

'He's been sidelined on the case, obviously; that's why I'm calling you. Sharpe's taken over the lead.'

'So what do you want me for?'

'He fits your profile perfectly and we need to know if you can work out where he could have gone. What would someone in his frame of mind be thinking? We've searched everywhere. I know it's a long shot, but he's had her now for nearly five hours and I'm worried we're going to be too late.'

'Give me the address of his house and I'll meet you there. I need to see where he lives, speak to his mother. Maybe there's somewhere that is special to him. I'll be with you as soon as I can.'

. . .

Saskia's own personal troubles were instantly forgotten as the image of Winter, devastated by his mother's disappearance, came into her mind. He was so close to his parents. It must be killing him that the man he was trying to catch had taken his own mother. She didn't waste a moment, Saskia downed a glass of water to help revive her brain and was in her car and driving to the east of the island and the home of Michael Rault within minutes.

Jonno met her outside the Rault house and signed her through the police cordon.

'Mrs Rault is in the sitting room, but she's not exactly being very cooperative. Refuses to answer half our questions. We've done a thorough search of the property,' Jonno said to her quietly as he led her into the house. 'You might want to go and take a look in the garden shed if you want to get an insight into his mind.'

Saskia did as Jonno suggested, keen to take a look at Michael's things before she questioned his mother. As they walked through the kitchen to the back door, she had a quick look in the cupboards. She saw exactly what she'd expected to find: a stack of canned soup.

The garden shed was not your average wooden storage place. It had been reinforced all round with metal grills and the door looked like it had been covered in sheet metal and then locked with three or four different bolts. Clearly Michael Rault did not want anyone getting in.

'We can't go in at the moment,' Jonno said to her, 'forensics are still working, but you can take a look from the door. It's an eye opener.'

Saskia took a deep breath and pulled the door open. It was surprisingly heavy, no doubt due to its reinforcement. As soon as she had it open, the smell hit her. A mix of rotting carcasses and formaldehyde. A white-suited forensics officer was bent over, collecting a sample of something on the floor.

The first thing that hit Saskia was that this was clearly Michael's safe place. These were his friends. A tatty dog sat by the armchair, which was clearly his, a budgie stood slightly lopsidedly on a shelf, looking – if you could call it that – towards his chair. Other creatures, a cat, rabbit, and another type of bird which was so badly taxidermized that she couldn't even tell what kind it was. All of them seemed to be looking towards his chair, like a throne. In here he was clearly the king, the one in charge, and by his side in a smaller armchair was the spike that Jonno had mentioned.

'Andrew,' Saskia greeted the back of the man still bent double on the floor. The forensics officer quickly stood up straight and turned around.

'Miss Monet.'

'Can I ask,' she said, 'are there any journals or notes, photographs or anything that he might have created other than these poor creatures?'

'Nothing like that in here,' Andrew said, frowning and looking around him. 'He liked his TV, the remote is well worn, although it could have been an older one taken from the house. I'd also say he regularly ate out here. Plenty of food debris around his chair. I mean can you imagine eating your dinner next to a corpse's head while being stared at by this lot?'

'I think this lot were his friends, this is his safe space, and while I haven't yet met his mother, I'm expecting to find her overbearing and controlling, so the victim's head with the sewn-up mouth was him asserting his control.'

Saskia said this as much to herself and Jonno as Andrew. She was thinking out loud, working through the psychology of Michael's character, the reasons for his behaviour, and most importantly where he might have gone.

Then as quickly as she'd walked up to the shed, she left and went back into the house. Jonno followed silently behind her.

She still didn't go into the sitting room where she knew

Michael's mother was, but instead went upstairs, opening a couple of doors until she found the room that was very obviously Michael's. Despite him being a grown man in his forties, Michael's bedroom could have passed for a child's room.

The wallpaper, although faded and damaged in several places, depicted old-fashioned racing cars. A corkboard was on the wall, smothered in tickets and leaflets from various attractions and shows in Jersey. She saw the Battle of Flowers, Jersey Air Show, Mont Orguiel Castle, and one that she could only just make out that said something about Fort Regent.

The rest of the room was immaculate. Michael had made his bed perfectly before he'd left, and everything was ordered and tidy. Too tidy in some ways; to Saskia, it indicated a person with obsessive compulsive disorder, most likely as a result of stress or anxiety. The person who slept in this bedroom was in complete contrast to the person who sat in the garden shed. In here he lived under a strict regime, controlled and anxious. Out there, he was free to do what he wanted and with whomever he wanted. He was the one in control. The question was why this split personality, because that could be the key to his whereabouts now.

Before she went downstairs, Saskia asked Jonno if she could look in the bedside cabinet and around the bed.

'Absolutely, but can I ask you to put these on?' Jonno said, handing her a pair of latex gloves.

Gloves on, Saskia crouched down and looked in the bedside cupboard. There wasn't much in there – some nail clippers, a hairbrush, and a copy of the Good Samaritan Bible, like the type you'd find in hotel rooms.

She picked that up and flicked through it, interested to see if there were any sections which had been particularly well read. The book fell open, not because it had been so well worn with reading, but because there was a polaroid wedged between the pages.

It showed a little boy with what Saskia presumed were his parents, all of them smiling and laughing close to what looked to be a fairground ride of some sort. She took it out. On the back was written 1983.

Saskia looked around the bedroom to see if she could find anything else that was personal, but found nothing.

'I'm going to take this downstairs to ask his mother about it,' she said to Jonno, 'it obviously means a lot to him. We need to find out what has caused his extreme personality behaviour. I'm under no doubt that the victims are surrogate mothers for him, but this photograph tells me that perhaps their relationship wasn't always like it is now. Be interesting to see if she'll tell me why it's changed.'

Saskia walked downstairs into the small living room that, like Michael's bedroom, looked as though it hadn't been decorated since the early 1990s. Sitting in an armchair by a small electric fire, was a woman in her mid to late seventies.

'Mrs Rault, this is Saskia Monet who is helping us with the inquiry,' Jonno said, introducing her.

The old woman looked Saskia up and down with an air of disgust and disapproval.

'Not another bloody person asking me questions. I've told you all I know. I don't know where he's gone. I wish you lot would just all get lost.'

'Hello, Mrs Rault.' Saskia smiled at her, moving some magazines so she could sit down in a chair opposite. 'I know that you wouldn't want any harm to come to the woman that Michael is with, so I just have a few questions that might help us to locate where they are.'

'I don't know this woman,' she spat back at Saskia, her face hard and unforgiving.

Saskia took her comment to be compliance, as she didn't say she wouldn't answer any questions. Rather than launch straight in, Saskia looked up at the photograph on the bookcase near

Mrs Rault. An image of a young happy woman who she presumed was her.

'That's a lovely photograph,' Saskia said, nodding to the picture.

Mrs Rault grunted.

'Is that you? You look very pretty in that dress, I bet you had your fair share of suitors.'

'Stop trying to butter me up, girl,' Mrs Rault replied. 'That was before I met my husband.'

Despite her biting back, Saskia could tell she was softening a little.

'I'm sorry, has your husband passed away?' she tested.

'He didn't die, he left us. Just upped and walked out when Michael was ten. Said he couldn't hack being a family man anymore. It was Michael's fault. He was too demanding, that's what it was.'

'That must have been very hard for you.'

'I survived. One less person to run around after.'

'It must have been hard for Michael too.'

'He was a nightmare afterwards, kept whining on and on about wanting to see his dad, so I told him: he doesn't want to see you. That's why he left.'

'Do you know if your ex-husband is still in the island?'

Mrs Rault shrugged. 'Doubt it.'

'Can you let us have his name and date of birth so Detective Vibert here can try to find out?'

'Good luck to you. Ian Rault, seventh July, 1946.'

'Thank you,' Saskia said. Beside her she saw Jonno texting the information to the team.

'I found this photograph of the three of you in Michael's room.'

Mrs Rault's head shot up, suddenly interested. 'I got rid of them all. Let me see that.' Saskia held it up to show her, but didn't hand it over, fearful that she could decide to tear it up.

'You had a good time as a family before he left, didn't you?' she continued.

'Did we? You know that, do you?'

'Well it certainly looks like you were having fun in the photograph. Did you go out as a family much?'

'We weren't drinkers if that's what you're asking.'

'No, I was meaning more day trips and visiting places around the island.'

'That was our last day out. He left us the next day,' Mrs Rault said, sneeringly. 'Obviously didn't have that much of a good time.'

Jonno approached her and held out his mobile phone for her to read a message.

Ian Rault, deceased in Ipswich, England, 2014.

She gave a small nod to Jonno. There was definitely no influence from the father in Michael's life.

'So, Michael was ten in this photo?'

'Yes I've told you that, are you simple?'

Saskia ignored her insults; she'd met and heard far worse.

'Looks like you enjoyed fairground rides together. Where is that, was it a travelling fair over for the Battle of Flowers?'

Saskia held up the photo to Mrs Rault and hoped she wouldn't just tell her to put it down again. The old woman squinted at the picture.

'No, you're too young to remember. That was Fort Regent. There was lots for kids to do up there in those days. Not like it is now, left to rot. They had all sorts of rides on the ramparts and an amusement arcade and roller skating. Michael used to love it. Didn't cost the earth to go either, not like they charge for everything nowadays.'

'Looks like it was a lot of fun,' Saskia said looking at the photograph. 'So this would have been the last time you had fun as a family together.'

Mrs Rault grunted. 'What are you asking me all these stupid questions for? Dragging up the past.'

'You blamed Michael for his father leaving. You became bitter and cold towards your son, a young boy who was just ten years old and couldn't understand why his father had left and his mother turned against him. The last time he would have experienced warmth and love was that day at Fort Regent, wasn't it?'

Saskia held up the polaroid image towards the sour-faced old woman in front of her.

Mrs Rault turned her cheek and looked the other way, but it didn't matter. Jonno had already left the room.

THIRTY-THREE

Winter was following the hunt for Michael Rault on the police radios. He'd gone back to the office after the raid on Michael Rault's house, desperate to be kept up to speed with developments. Every time somebody radioed back that they hadn't found anything or anyone, his heart plummeted. How long would Michael keep his mother alive? Where could he be holding her?

Then he got a text from Jonno.

> Saskia thinks Rault might be up at Fort Regent.
> Where the old fun rides used to be.

Winter grabbed his police radio and was out the office within seconds. He could be at Fort Regent in minutes.

When Winter arrived, there were other officers in the car park having a quick meeting before they set off. He knew it was the right thing to do, come up with a systematic search plan, but he was beyond that. He parked well away from them so they didn't notice his arrival and then he ran into the building and headed for the exit where he knew he'd be able to access the ramparts.

It was a big site with a myriad of small rooms and places to hide. Originally an old Fort, as the name suggests, it was built in the early 1800s on the hill above St Helier. In modern times, a dome was put on top and it was converted into a leisure centre, but now it was little used while it waited for a redevelopment plan to be decided by the government.

Winter ran up the concrete steps and out onto the external areas. He didn't want to frighten Rault into doing anything in haste, so he walked as quietly as he could, being careful as he came to corners. It was a desolate sight, a once vibrant building now looking neglected and sad. Nature's graffiti in green with the local kids having added their own artwork. It was a long way from its halcyon days. Winter had been racking his brains trying to remember if there was anything dolmen-like up here. Some particular place that Michael would go to that was similar to the other dolmens. He remembered that there'd been one removed from the site when the Fort was built, but that was now in some celebrity's back garden in the UK after being given to a former governor. There was nothing else that he could think of that was still here.

Winter was listening to the police radio and so knew that the team he'd seen in the car park were on their way up, and so far their search had found nothing. Winter had covered a fair section of the ramparts and was beginning to wonder if Saskia had got it wrong again. After all, she'd been so sure about the prison officer being involved. It was perfectly feasible that she might have got this wrong too. Rault and Winter's mother could be anywhere in Jersey.

As he walked around, the wind picked up on the seaward side and it was harder to hear if there were any other people up here. He was just about to round a corner, when he thought he heard voices.

He stopped, straining to catch again what he'd just heard.

The wind pushed the sounds away again and then gusted them back to him.

It was a man's voice, and a woman's. His mother.

Winter crept closer.

'Do you remember the aquarium? I used to love going there, it was so relaxing watching the fish.'

'The rays were my favourite,' the male voice now, quieter.

'Such a shame that it's all gone now. I do like the butterfly exhibit up at the zoo though, do you go there at all? It's nice and warm in there and the butterflies will land on you. They're beautiful, so fragile.'

'Not really. Maybe we can go there one day.'

'Yes, of course we can, why not. What are your favourite animals?'

Winter heard the forced cheerfulness in his mother's voice and the tension in her throat had raised the tone slightly, but he was relieved to hear how calm she sounded.

Should he walk up to them, or would that scare Rault? Part of him, the son, wanted to rush straight up to them now and grab his mother. Protect her. But the police detective, the professional who had dealt with volatile situations before, knew caution was his best friend. He walked back a few yards and whispered into his radio to tell the rest of the team that he'd found them. A minute later, he was joined by six of his colleagues.

Winter had peered around the corner of the Fort to look at where his mother and Rault were. They were sat, looking out over the town as though they were there for a stroll and a chat. He told the commanding officer what he'd seen.

'We've got officers getting into position on the other side. You say this guy's an honorary?'

Winter nodded.

'We'll use that to our advantage then, get one of the team to be strolling by and pretend to recognise him, strike up a conversation. With him distracted, we can get your mother away quickly.'

It was a solid plan, but would it work? The commanding officer was a good bloke. Winter knew he led his team well and they got results. He had to believe that they were going to be successful again today.

'I'm going to have to ask you to stay well back though, sir,' the sergeant added. 'Strict orders that you are not to engage.' He looked at him with raised eyebrows, but sympathetic eyes.

Winter knew Sharpe would have given that order, worried that Winter might lose it with their suspect. The man had a good point. Right now with the way every single molecule in his body felt like it was on fire, he couldn't guarantee that he wouldn't do something he might later regret. He nodded his agreement, but it was going to be hard.

Winter crept back to his position from where he could hear the conversation still, but was well out of the way of the operation.

'You know we should be getting back,' he heard his mother say. 'It's beginning to get a bit cold up here.'

There was silence for a few moments, then, 'You're going to reject me like the others, aren't you? You're all the same.'

'No, don't be silly, I'm not going to reject you,' his mother replied, but Winter heard the change in her voice. She was scared now.

Every muscle in his body itched to pounce. To run straight in there and help her.

Then he heard another voice, it was one of their team.

'Oh, hi, Michael, isn't it?' the officer said. 'We met at some demonstration, didn't we? You're an honorary right?'

'Yes. I don't remember you.'

'Really? We all went for a few beers after, don't you remember that?'

'What demonstration was it?'

But Michael didn't get his answer because Winter heard the sound of running feet, a grunt as he suspected somebody had floored Michael Rault followed by an officer announcing that he was under arrest, and a 'Thank goodness' from his mother.

Winter couldn't wait any longer – he rushed round the corner to find her.

She was there, being led towards him by two officers. She looked pale and she looked tired, but all Winter cared about was that she was alive and unharmed.

Her face burst into a smile as she saw him.

'I'm so sorry,' he said taking her into a huge hug. 'I should have come round, taken more notice of your phone calls.'

'It's alright. It's my fault too, I should have been more patient. Is Enid alright? I've been so worried about her.'

'They think she'll be fine. She was lucky to have you as a friend because I don't think she'd still be fine if you hadn't gone round there.'

Winter watched as Michael Rault was handcuffed and read his rights. He looked again at the man he'd met at the station just yesterday and wondered how he could have done what he did to two innocent women.

'I need to call your father, he'll be worried sick,' his mother said to him.

'Yes of course,' Winter said, pulling out his mobile and dialling his parent's home number. 'You know I couldn't believe how calm you were. I heard you chatting. You get kidnapped by a man who has already killed two women and you reminisce about an old aquarium!'

'I knew you would come, that's why. It was obvious what Michael wanted. He's a very mixed-up man, but he just wants his mother to love him. I gave him what he wanted until you turned up.'

'Well, I can see where I get it from.' Winter laughed, the

relief making his legs and hands shake as the adrenaline wore off. Then his father's worried voice came to him from his mobile.

'Dad, I've got someone you might want to talk to,' he said and handed his phone over to his mother.

THIRTY-FOUR

Winter arrived at Saskia's cottage with a bottle of wine. He had already made up his mind what he was going to say if David Carter was there again, he'd just tell her that he'd brought it round as a thank you for helping find his mother.

When she opened the door, he instantly knew she was alone.

'Winter!' she said.

'Sorry, I know I should have called but, well, I left in a hurry last time I was here and so I thought I'd claim that pizza if it's still going.'

She smiled. 'It is, come on in.'

'I wanted to thank you for helping find my mother. You were spot on about Fort Regent. Jonno told me that Mrs Rault would never have told us any of that if you hadn't teased it out of her.'

'I'm just glad your mum's OK,' Saskia replied, getting two glasses for the wine.

'Yes. Any longer and it may have been too late.' Winter stopped himself. He didn't want to think about that so he changed the subject. 'Mark Byrne was charged with causing suffering to animals. We found three cats buried in his garden, along with various wildlife. Plus we have some charges likely in relation to extreme pornography. I understand that he's been suspended from the prison so you're not going to get bothered by him again.'

'That's a relief; I have to be honest it was worrying me that he might have found out who it was that got you involved. He deserves as much as you can throw at him. I keep seeing that poor little cat fly through the air after he'd shot it.'

'He thinks it's the neighbours who reported him so you're off the hook on that one. I also want to clear the air,' Winter continued. He felt emboldened by the day's events – thinking you might lose your mother could have that effect. 'What you do in your spare time is your business, I don't need any explanations. It's good working with you and I can accept that if it's what you want.'

Saskia stopped what she was doing and turned to face him.

'There are some things you need to know, Winter. I've not been totally honest with you.'

He couldn't help it, but he felt the dejection hit him full on. He'd never seen her look so solemn before. She seemed to take a big breath before she continued.

'My birth name is actually Saskia Carter. David Carter is my brother. The reason I changed my name is because our father is Edward Carter who was convicted of the murders of seven women in the UK. The Nightingale Strangler they called him. He also nearly killed our mother but I called the police and had him arrested before he could. My father is a psychopath. The prison service knows my history. It's been the impetus for my career.' Saskia said. Then she paused, her eyes searching his face, clearly trying to assess Winter's reaction.

It was certainly a day for drama.

'Wow, OK, that must have been a tough childhood,' Winter

said, not really sure what he should say to that news. He was shocked but actually what he really felt was relief.

'So David isn't your boyfriend?'

'No. Absolutely not.'

'OK.' Winter didn't know what to say next. All the times that she'd clammed up whenever he talked about her family and her childhood now made total sense.

'I understand if you decide you don't want to use me for profiling anymore,' Saskia said to him.

He looked into her eyes and saw for the first time a vulnerability which she'd never shown before. She was baring her soul to him and all he could say was *wow*. He could imagine Jonno's disapproving face.

'I think you're amazing,' he said. 'To have had such a tough childhood and to then turn that around into a career where you make a difference, that's quite remarkable. Why would we stop using you? I couldn't think of anyone more qualified.'

Saskia said nothing, her eyes brimmed with tears and she looked away.

'Thank you,' she whispered.

Winter could feel the electricity between them, pulling them into each other. He wanted to reach out and hold her, kiss her, but he daren't.

'After you kissed me the other night,' he started, 'I should have been honest with you too, about my feelings. I was glad that you'd done it, but I couldn't understand why you'd suddenly stopped.'

She looked at him quizzically.

'I'm the daughter of a convicted psychopath. I didn't think that exactly makes me ideal girlfriend material.'

'Your family history doesn't change how I feel about you. You're not your father. I've already told you I think you're incredible, it's just made me respect you even more.'

'Really?'

'Really. I'm the son of a civil servant who thinks exciting means watching *Gardeners' World*, but that's not who I am.'

Saskia allowed herself to smile.

Winter reached for her hand and pulled her closer. There were no barriers between them now. Their bodies melded together as they both held on to each other, weeks and months of longing on their lips.

'Oh, and by the way,' Winter said, pausing briefly to look at her, 'Mum's invited you for Sunday lunch. She wants to say thank you herself.'

THIRTY-FIVE

David drove home from work expecting to find Jackie waiting for him. She'd said that she was going to speak to the lawyer about getting him added to her company board and he was trying to hurry that along without it looking like he was pressurising her. He stopped on the way home to buy her some flowers.

When he arrived at the house, he found the gates wouldn't open. He swore. The code wasn't working; there must have been a fault. He rang Jackie's mobile.

'Sweetheart, there's a fault with the gates, could you open them manually for me?'

'There's no fault, David. Wait there.'

He stood in the beam of his car headlights, light rain just beginning to slant down from the sky, wondering what was going on. He watched as Jackie walked up to the gates, a man following a discreet way behind.

'This is Lester, Allan's replacement,' she said to David when she saw his puzzled look. To David he looked more like a bodyguard than a driver, but he said nothing. Something was going on and he didn't like it.

'Lester is going to give you your stuff; I've packed it into three suitcases. We are finished, David. I know what your game plan is and I know that you don't love me at all, you're not capable of loving. The free rent and board has come to an end and I don't want you trying to contact me or any of my friends ever again. Is that clear?'

'What's happened, Jackie? Why are you being like this? All I've ever done is try to love you and look after you.' He tried to sound innocent and upset by her words.

'Quit the bullshit, David. It's over.' With that she turned and walked back to the house. The man she'd called Lester picked up three suitcases stacked by the gate pillar and passed them through to David without a word.

David took them and loaded them into his car, his blood boiling. He would have thought that perhaps he'd overdone the pressure on Jackie to sign things over to him, or maybe she'd begun to suspect that he was gaslighting her and drugging her drinks. But he knew that wasn't it. He knew exactly what had upset Jackie. 'You're not capable of loving,' she'd said to him. There was only one person in this island who would know that: his sister, Saskia.

A LETTER FROM THE AUTHOR

Dear reader,

Thank you so much for choosing to read *Island of Graves*, the third in the Saskia Monet series. I hope you are enjoying going on the journey with Saskia, Winter, and David, as well as the amazing backdrop of Jersey. If you want to join other readers in hearing all about my new Storm releases, you can sign up here:

www.stormpublishing.co/gwyn-bennett

I also have my own readers' club, with a free novella and other bonuses including competitions. deleted scenes, and news of all my latest releases. It's free to sign up at: www.gwynbennett.com You can unsubscribe any time, but it would be great to keep in touch.

If you enjoyed this book and could spare a few moments to leave a review that would be hugely appreciated. Even a short review can make all the difference in encouraging a reader to discover my books for the first time. Thank you so much!

The inspiration for Island of Graves comes from the history and landscape of the Channel Island of Jersey. The dolmens which feature in this book, are real. There are around a dozen of them dotted around the island, six-thousand-year-old structures created by our ancestors. La Hougue Bie, in particular, is small but spectacular, and carries the scars and additions made by subsequent generations over the millennia. Well worth a visit if you're ever in the island, but I hope you don't bump into a severed head as you crawl into the chamber!

Thank you again for choosing to read one of my books. I do love to hear from readers and you can find me on social media and at my website, gwynbennett.com, where you can also sign up to my free readers club and receive a free novella. I have many more stories and characters to entertain you with, so I hope you'll stay on the journey with me, Saskia and some of the other people who regularly inhabit my head.

Happy reading

Gwyn Bennett

- facebook.com/GwynGBwriter
- x.com/GwynGB
- instagram.com/gwyngb
- amazon.com/author/gwynbennett
- bookbub.com/authors/gwyn-bennett

ACKNOWLEDGEMENTS

A big thank you to the whole team at Storm who have helped bring this book to you. In particular, Kathryn Taussig, my publisher, Natasha Hodgson and Shirley Khan for their editing and proofreading, and Eileen Carey for the fabulous cover. There's also the brilliant Caitlin Shannon who narrates the audio books.

Most of all, thank you for coming on this reading journey with me and I hope you'll stay in touch.

Printed in Dunstable, United Kingdom